Extremities

STORIES

EXTREMITIES

STORIES BY Kathe Koja

Four Walls Eight Windows

NEW YORK / LONDON

© 1998 Kathe Koja

Published in the United States by
Four Walls Eight Windows
39 West 14th Street, room 503
New York, NY 10011
http://www.fourwallseightwindows.com

U.K. offices:
Four Walls Eight Windows/Turnaround
Unit 3 Olympia Trading Estate
Coburg Road, Wood Green
London N22 67Z

First printing September 1998.

Library of Congress Cataloguing-in-Publication Data:
Koja, Kathe.
    Extremities : stories / Kathe Koja.
       p.   cm.
    ISBN: 1-56858-122-X
    I. Title.
    PS3561.O376E9   1998
    813'.54—dc21   98-20327
    CIP

The stories were originally published in the following publications: "Angels in Love," *Fantasy & Science Fiction* (1991); "Arrangement for Invisible Voices," *Dark Voices* (1993); "Bird Superior," *Asimov's* (1991); "Ballad of the Spanish Civil Guard," *Alternative Warriors* (1995); "The Company of Storms," *Fantasy & Science Fiction* (1992); "The Disquieting Muse," *Little Deaths* (1994); "Illusions in Relief," *Pulphouse* (1990); "Jubilee," *Ghosts* (1995); "Lady Lazarus," *Fantasy & Science Fiction* (1996); "The Neglected Garden," *Fantasy & Science Fiction* (1991); "Pas de Deux," *Dark Love* (1995); "Queen of Angels," *Omni* (1994); "Teratisms," *A Whisper of Blood* (1991); "Waking the Prince," *Ruby Slippers, Golden Tears* (1995).

10 9 8 7 6 5 4 3 2 1
Printed in Canada
Text design by Ink, Inc., New York, New York

CONTENTS

For Rick

Arrangement for Invisible Voices

MIDNIGHT, and the spread and shift of Laurah's thighs beneath him. Hold it. Hold onto it. Olson grunts, almost comically loud, urging himself onward, inward, harder, willing himself to hear nothing but the warm creak of moving flesh, the building tension of his breath. Don't listen. *Do not listen,* but it's already too late, he can hear them, unbearable tender wail of their murdered cries, scaling like the scream of high opera and he's slowing, slacking, Laurah's hands rise vicious on his sweaty back but it's no use, it's too late, it's been too late for weeks now. He flops down upon her, sorrow and shame, her lips twist into movement but he can hear nothing, not the ugly names she calls him, idiot, crazy man. Only the cries, songs, the noises of the pigs.

He dresses, same vaguely smelly clothes of the day, while Laurah lies in the circle of bedside light and pointedly masturbates, staring at him with such hatred that he can feel it even when his back is turned. He knows she is right to hate him, can meet it with nothing but silence; a stoic macho silence would be best, of course, but in his case he can summon only a sort of self-despising wordlessness, telling her that he hates himself as much as she does, but with less verve. The very slouch he uses to leave the room tells her something. He hopes.

There's half a tank in the car. Midnight blue Ford with a starter problem, ho ho, don't start with *me*. He drives for over an hour before pulling into the parking lot of a bar called the Satellite Lounge, he has learned it's best to park where there are other cars. Reaching into the glove box, noticing in a distant way that he has almost overcome his furtiveness, he looks only twice over his shoulder before extracting the headless Barbie doll. Cold fingers a loose *o* around her tiny waist, he gazes at the smooth plastic bulb of her neck and says, "You know, I really can't believe this." And laughs: what is it, exactly, that you don't believe? That your wife despises you for a madman, that your ears ache with the screams of dead animals, that your only confidant is a child's discarded toy? You got a problem with that?

He laughs again, rubs one despairing finger on the jut of Barbie's left breast. "Let's go grab some barbecue," he says.

That fucking barbecue. Laurah had been against the idea, of course, and he had worn her down into it, again of course. "You're like a hillful of ants," Laurah had said, dressing, pissed-off shimmy into cool blue clothes. "A grain here, a grain there, and pretty soon everything's a desert." Why it had been so important to attend, he not only remembered but could not forget: he had never been to a real old-fashioned pig roast before. Pig roast barbecue, shimmer on the stick, yum yum. As if, curiousto witness an execution, he had found himself upon arrival the victim of choice.

Laurah's surface frost had turned to graciousness, for public consumption only but it was pleasant enough that Olson could relax a little, enjoy the talk, have a drink. He remembered standing in the warming shade, watching the glimmer of the fire, watched too with a kind of primitive childlike pleasure, little boy poking roadkill with a wondering stick, as the three small (and they were small) roasting pigs were carried to the circle of the pits.

A few minutes only, he was still sipping his second drink

when he heard it: an uneasy sound, not tickle but scrape in his ear. Uncomfortable he smiled, listened harder to the talk or tried to but the sound grew louder, the unmistakable sound of singing, crying. Embarrassed, yes, scared too a little but there was no ignoring it, it soared through the talk like a scream through mutters, actually piercing, his ears felt bruised from the pressure, his auditory canal seemed to swell, what in God's name is going *on* and then, rising an order of magnitude so there was no longer even the possibility of concealing its effect, he fell to his knees, buckling like punched, the singing scream no longer an expression of pain but pain itself and possessed at the same time of a beauty so eerie and fierce that while he pounded at his ears to stop the sound he was obscurely glad he could not, even to this very moment was glad he had not.

It was coming from the pigs. Spitted bodies, split bellies dull and glowing from the fire beneath, feet tied like victims, their eyes were alive, alive, and though their small hairy mouths moved not at all the song continued to grow, to burn as they burned. Yet it was not, and he knew this, not their own prosaic torment that they mourned, oh no something large, large, some huge death celebrated in accusatory song.

Crying, whining through his open mouth while Laurah stood there gaping and warm with fearful surprise, shame, what was on her face then he could not really say, nor say how many others beside him knelt or lay, pointed toward the roasting, weeping or silent or biting at their own hands; one woman's jaw had somehow spasmed, her teeth almost severing her own thumb, he remembered hearing, soft and distant, her screams of mingled sorrow and self-inflicted pain. The heat from the pits was choking him, was he screaming, too, clawing at his clothing, did anyone hear him?

He did not recall the song stopping, only that it had

stopped, and he curled to fetal, a dull wet circle growing at his crotch; and Laurah, staring at him.

A relief to blame it, however lamely, on hallucination, mass temporary madness, something, but the sound was a fact: even the ones who had not heard the singing had heard *something,* one man called it a whine like bad cassette tape, another like the sound a mosquito makes. Even Laurah had been touched by it. She wept, driving home, mucus thin on her upper lip, that sweet pucker he loved, her hands clenching and unclenching on the wheel. Mile after mile of denial that turned somehow to accusation, fury, a cold disbelief that anything but a sort of group hysteria had taken place, one nut feeding off another, I don't know what it was but I'll tell you one thing I don't want to hear about it any more.

"How can you say that," incredulous, his own brand of disbelief, "you were there," but no, her anger blossomed hotter, lasted a full day after he had ceased to bring it up, melted finally to a sullen warmth that accepted him into her arms.

The moment of entry, her breath on his neck and the feel of her, his hips poised and then like a blow, the vicious flip of an unnamed switch, came the incredible song, horrifying, lush, stunning him so he fell atop her, felt her scrambling struggle away as he grabbed at his ears and cried.

Crying still, three weeks later, weeping to Barbie while at home Laurah lay comparing the costs of lawyers and psychiatrists. Beneath the seat, cool stare up through his worthless crotch to his very heart, the Barbie's head: her eyes are Laurah's blue so in a rash moment he popped her head off, he wants in fact to throw the head away but is obscurely afraid he will someday be confronted with its lack so thus, post-decapitation, into the backseat, where it slipped under the front seat, matte pink lips slam kissed by rolling oblivious Pepsi bottles and the window scraper performing occasional toothless surgery, he feels vaguely guilty about the whole thing. Still she, it, his only friend, the comforting slick feel of her plastic legs in his hand, to whom else can he tell his tale of musical apocalypse, who else gives a shit.

Her legs are still warm in his hand as he circles the car around, heads back, sweat perking brighter in his armpits the closer he gets to home, the radio tuned to the all-talk station, loud, loud, loud.

A discussion with Laurah is a spectacularly bad idea in both theory and practice, but he tries; pathetic, but he tries. Gently cornering her, cloaking his supplicant's terror in what he hopes passes for irony: what does she think, looking and not looking at her, about what's been happening?

"What's been happening?" There is no irony in *her*, no terror either it seems; with the iron smile of mockery she tells him nothing has been happening, which would seem to be the problem. His problem. She makes this painfully clear, if he is going to dress his impotence in madman's motley she wants no part of it, will certainly not discuss it, and in fact has doubts that it is even worth discussing. She walks away, leaving him wide-eyed at her matter-of-fact brutality. Yet later in the evening, making a sandwich with the remains of the curled up bologna, he hears her weeping, weeping in the spare bathroom, he can picture her there: shoulder pressed against the door, one short-nailed hand fisted to her mouth, a child's posture of pain. He cries as he pounds the sandwich to a glue of meat and bread, then wipes his face with a paper towel, scratchy like newsprint, some fucking country home motif, just what country did you have in mind?

There is no talk between them for the rest of the night;

he does not say that he heard her grief. Yet as they lie in that cold trench of silence, that marital bed, she grasps him, hands almost painful in their need, covers his smile with her wet mouth; atop him, rubbing, pushing, working him like a beautiful tool, he is hard with her passion, he is inside her, stroking busily away and her own hips bucking, stropping, and oh please, oh no but yes, the freight-train murmur of the hellish song, its pain is his and he deflates, Laurah is shouting, elbows jammed in the pillow beneath his head: "God *damn* it!" and rolls off and away from him, his small defeated penis slipping from her like some useless apology. In his private pain he cannot even speak, and later, wrung with that other consumption, he is too ashamed to. He does not sleep, at all, at all, and does not dare to ask her if she does.

Laurah will no longer let him touch her. He is somewhat glad about this and still profoundly sorry, but inside a hope twitches, perhaps they'll let him alone now, perhaps he won't hear them anymore. And—is it?—a tickle of regret as well, but a worthy sacrifice, he will do without the beauty if he can only somehow get his life back. Moses in the desert, that bush is *not* burning, no. She goes to bed early, he stays up late, drinking warmish beer, wakes on the sofa with a headache and a lightening heart.

This lasts for nearly two full weeks, twelve days to be exact. Homeward march, stalled to a crawl beneath a sunset like roasted pork and oh my God so much *louder* now, howling, angels' cacophony, he drags the wheel to at least get off the road and all his skin ashiver, the sound true pain now, pain in his own flesh, crying aloud to stop it, please stop it, oh please just stop. Afterwards his tired hands find the furrows dug into his cheeks, abrasions twinned to the skinless tips of his fingers, Rorschach blood all over. He tries to clean up with glove box tissues, the bare Barbie hips somehow sardonic as they lay pouted towards him, the tissue clinging damp to his fingers so he rolls it down to little bloody balls, which he flicks to the floor. It takes him nearly an hour to get the rest of the way home.

Laurah, sudden stare of worry and surprise hardening almost at once to a kind of nervous hate, what's the nut up to now. He goes upstairs, he will lie down, rest somehow. Did he even sleep before it starts up again, crawling round and round the bedroom, chin pressed to the floor, dry lips open in a scream that is in some distorted way an echo of their song. When he truly wakes Laurah is not home, past midnight and she is not home. Gone maybe to fetch a twenty-four-hour shrink, call a cop, whatever. The song rises to assault pitch only once more that night, but it never now departs; always in his head the constant mutter, barely coasting subliminal but there, subtle like the endless drift of blood through his veins, as beyond his conscious reining as the nameless dance of neurons in his brain.

Laurah does not come home. He calls in sick, vomits briefly, goes back to bed. Around two thirty, the sun a dull slant through the back kitchen window, he eats half a cup of vegetable soup, his hands trembling shivers, elegant tympani, against the lip of the heavy blue cup. The song continues.

Night. Laurah has not come home, will most likely never come home, why should she. "Why should she?" asking the Barbie, she's a woman isn't she, girl talk, what's the scoop. Dear Ann Landers, my husband is losing his mother-fucking mind. How about the others, there, at the barbecue, the blood roast, have they all gone crazy too, what about that woman who bit off her own thumb? Dead, I know they are, all of them, one by one, crazy from the sound and then dead, stiff, corpses, worm food, "Oh my God I didn't even eat any, I didn't even *eat* any!" to the silent kitchen as the sun runs lower and the soup pours like some ominous new fluid across the long field of the table, drips onto his pant legs, onto his shoes as cool and slick as hooves.

Laurah's hands shake, she is determined, she wants to cry but will not allow herself. Doctor Ted beside her is trying to be soothing, keep a light touch; wait, she wants to say, we'll see how ironic you think all this is, just wait, you'll see.

Through the dark house, now she's really scared, Ted's gravity gone to a flat-eyed calm as they look, search, Laurah wondering if now is the moment, Olson with a hatchet like some stupid slasher but oh, it could happen, it could be, see the way the soup is clotted there, see the greasy shine of it in the kitchen light that looks so weak, now, so pale against the darker cast of some tragedy that is looming like movie doom only worse of course because it's—

From the backyard. Singing. Olson, singing. Past Ted, her heart is beating so hard it's hard to run, out the back door to see Olson, on his knees, a flashlight circle burned to full dim, scraping at the ground with, what. What? Pink and plastic. Oh God, oh shit, it's a doll, a Barbie doll. Digging a trench with a Barbie doll by the light of the midnight moon, singing, only this time Olson, crazy now for sure and oh, serene? Yes, sweet monk's smile and all, his pant legs rich with dirt, dirt up to his elbows, and Barbie, well, of course she's looked better.

"Olson."

He shakes his head at her, not menacing, keeps singing. Louder. Louder, almost shouting, my God what a horrible sound and stupid Ted beside her keeps repeating

"What's he saying, what's he *saying*," as if she knows. Olson's eyes almost closed in the dim light of his burning-out flash, him too, and tears come to her as she realizes just how crazy this actually is and "Stop it" she cries to him, reaches to touch him but never does as a sound blows out of his throat, knocks him sideways to half-scrabble for his Barbie as from his open body comes the vortex of the pigs' cantata, the skies full of the holy noise, not only the cries of the dying but the screaming of the murdered, oh Jesus God she can hear it, she can hear it too. And Ted there, mouth open, moving, he's talking, she can't hear a word he says.

The Neglected Garden

"I DON'T WANT TO GO," she said. "I'm not going."
Patient and calm, the way he wanted to be, he explained again; they had discussed it, she was moving out. He had already packed her things for her, five big cardboard boxes, labeled, he had done the best he could. Clothes on hangers and her big Klee print wrapped and tied carefully across with string, everything neatly stacked in the car, here, he said, here's the keys.

"I don't want the car," she said. Tears ran down her face but she made no crying sounds, her breathing did not change, in fact her expression did not change. She stood there staring at him with rolling tears and her hands empty, palms upwards, at her sides. He kissed her, a little impatiently, on her mouth.

"You have to go," he said. "Please, Anne, we've gone all through this. Let's not make it any harder than it already is," although in fact it wasn't all that hard, not for him anyway. "Please," and he leaned forward but did not kiss her again; her lips were unpleasantly wet.

She stared at him, saying nothing. He began to feel more than impatient, angry in fact, but no, he would say nothing too, he would give as good as he got. He put her car keys in her hand, literally closing her fingers around them, and picking up his own keys left the house. An hour or so, he would come back and she would be gone.

When he got back her car was still in the driveway, but

she was nowhere in the house, not upstairs, not in the utility room; nowhere. Feeling a little silly, he looked in the closets, even considered looking under the bed; nothing. "Anne," calling her, louder and louder, "Anne, stop it, where are you," walking through the house and a movement, something in the backyard, caught his eye through the big kitchen windows. Letting the screen door slam, hard, walking fast and then seeing her, stopping as if on the perilous lip of a fire.

She was on the fence. The back fence, old now and leaning, half its braces gone. She sat at the spot where the rotted wood ended and the bare fencing began, legs straight out, head tipped just slightly to the right. Her arms were spread in a loose posture of crucifixion, and through the flesh of her wrists she had somehow pierced the rusty wire of the fence, threading it around the tendons, the blood rich and thick and bright like some strange new food and while he stood there staring and staring a fly settled down on the blood and walked around in it, back and forth.

He kept staring at the fly, it was suddenly so hot in the yard, it was as if he couldn't see, or could see only half of the scene before him, a kind of dazzle around the perimeters of his vision like the beginning of a fainting fit and back and forth went the fly, busy little black feet and he screamed "Son of a *bitch!*" and moved to slap the fly away, and as his hand touched the wound she gave a very small sound, and he pulled his hand back and saw the blood on it.

He said something to her, something about my God Anne what the hell and she opened her eyes and looked at him in a slow considering kind of way, but with a certain blankness as if she viewed him now from a new perspective, and another fly landed and more hesitantly he brushed that one away, and still she did not speak at all.

"You have to go to the hospital," he told her. "You're bleeding, it's dangerous to bleed that way."

She ignored him by closing her eyes. Ants were walking over her bare feet. She didn't seem to feel them. "Anne," loudly, "I'm calling an ambulance, I'm calling the police, Anne."

The police were not helpful. He would have to press charges, they said, trespass charges against her to have her removed. They became more interested when he started to explain, in vague halting phrases, exactly how she was attached to his fence, and in sudden nervous fear he hung up, perhaps they would think he had done it to her himself, who knew what Anne might tell them, she was obviously crazy, to do that to herself she would have to be crazy. He looked out the kitchen window and saw her looking at the house, her eyes tracking as he moved slowly past the windows. He didn't know what to do. He sat in the living room and tried to think.

By the time the sun went down he still had no idea what course to take. He did not even want to go back outside but he did, stood looking down at her. "Do you want some water? Or some aspirin or something?" and in the same breath enraged by what he had just said, the extreme and dangerous stupidity of the whole situation, he shouted at her, called her a stupid fucking idiot and walked back inside, shaking, shaking in his legs and knees and inside his body, felt his heart pounding, it was hard to breathe. She had to be in pain. Was she so crazy she didn't even feel pain anymore? Maybe it was a temporary thing, temporary insanity, maybe a night spent outside would shock her out of it, a night sitting on the cold ground.

In the morning she was still there, although she had stopped bleeding. Ants walked up and down her legs. The blood at her wrists had clotted to jelly. The skin of her face was very white.

"Anne," he said, and shook his head. Her hair was damp, parts of it tangled in the fence, and the pulse in her throat beat so he could see it, a sluggish throb. He felt sorry for her, he hated her. He wanted her to just get up and go away. "Anne, please, you're not doing yourself any good, this is hurting you," and the look she gave him then was so pointed that he felt his skin flush, he refused to say anything, he turned and went back into the house.

Someone was knocking at his front door: the woman from next door, Barbara something, joined by the paperboy's mother whose name he could not remember. They were shrill, demanding to know what he was going to do about that poor woman out there and my God this and that and he shouted at them from the depths of his confusion and anger, told them to get the hell off his porch and he had already been in contact with the police if that would satisfy them, thank you very much, it's none of your business to start with. When they had gone he sat down, he felt very dizzy all of a sudden, he felt as if he had to sit down for awhile, a good long while.

How, he didn't know, but he fell asleep, there in the chair, woke with his shirt collar sticking to his neck, sweat on his forehead and above his upper lip. He felt chilled. As he went into the kitchen to get something warm to drink his gaze went to the windows, it was irresistible, he had to look.

She was still there, slumped back against the fence, a curve in her arms and back that curiously suggested tension. She saw him; he knew it by the way her body moved, just a little, as his cautious figure came into view. He ducked away, then felt embarrassed somehow, as if he had been caught peeping in a window, then angry at himself and almost instantly at her.

Let her sit, he said to himself. We'll see who gets tired of this first.

It was almost ten days later that he called a doctor, a friend of his. Anne had not moved, he had barely gone near her, but even his cursory window inspections showed him things were changing, it was nothing he wanted to have to inspect. After much debate he called Richard, told him there was a medical situation at his house; his evasiveness puzzled Richard who said, "Look, if you have somebody sick there, you'd be better off getting her to a hospital. It is a her, isn't it?" Yes, he said. I just need you to come over here, he said, it's kind of a situation, you'll know what I mean when you see her.

Finally Richard arrived, and he directed him straight out to the back yard, stood watching from the window, drinking a glass of ice water. Richard was back in less than five minutes, his face red. He slammed the screen door hard behind him.

"I don't know what the hell's going on here," Richard said, "but I'll tell you one thing, that woman out there is in bad shape, I mean bad shape. She's got an infection that—"

Well, he said, you're a doctor, right?

"I'm a gynecologist," and Richard was shouting now. "She belongs in a hospital. This is criminal, this is a criminal situation. That woman could die from this."

He drank a little of his ice water, a slow swallow, and Richard leaned forward and knocked the glass right out of his hand. "I said she could die from this, you asshole, and I'm also saying that if she does it's your fault."

"My fault? My fault, how can it be my fault when she's

the one who—" but Richard was already leaving, slamming back out the door, gone. The ice water lay in a glossy puddle on the chocolate-colored tile. He looked out the window. Her posture was unchanged.

It was a kind of dream, less nightmare than sensation of almost painful confusion, and he woke from it sweaty, scared a little, sat up to turn on the bedside lamp. It was almost three. He put on a pair of khaki jeans and walked barefoot into the backyard, the flashlight set on dim, a wavering oval of pale yellow light across the grass.

Perhaps she was asleep.

He leaned closer, not wanting to come too close but wanting to see, and flicked the light at her face.

Moths were walking across her forehead, pale as her skin, a luminous promenade. A small sound came from him as she opened her eyes. There was a moth beneath her right eyelid. It looked dead.

Her hair was braided into the fence, and the puffy circles of infection at her wrists had spread, a gentle bloat extending almost to her elbows. There was a slightly viscous shine to the original wounds. The old blood there had a rusty tinge. The grass seemed greener now, lapping at her bare feet and ankles. When he touched her with the light she seemed almost to feel it, for she turned her head, not away from the light as he expected but into it, as if it was warm and she was cold.

No doubt she was cold. If he touched her now—

He flicked the light to full power, a small brassy beam, played it up and down her body, nervously at first then with more confidence as she moved so little, so gently in its light. Her hair looked dark as a vine. There was dew on her clothing. He stood looking at her for it seemed to him a very long time, but when he returned to the house he saw it was barely quarter after three.

She kept on changing. The infection worsened and then apparently stabilized; at least it spread no farther. Her arms, a landscape of green and pale brown, leaves and the supple wood of the creeping growth about her breasts and waist, her clothing paler and more tattered, softly stained by the days of exposure. Flowers were starting to sprout behind her head, strange white flowers like some distorted stylized nimbus, Our Lady of the Back Forty. Her feet were a permanent green. It seemed her toenails were gone.

None of the neighbors would talk to him now. His attempts at explanations, bizarre even to his own ears, turned them colder still. Each day after work he would look through the kitchen windows, each day he would find some new change, minute perhaps but recognizable. It occurred to him that he was paying her more attention than ever now, and in a moment of higher anger he threw a tarp over her, big and blue and plastic, remnant of boating days. It smelled. He didn't care. She smelled too, didn't she? He covered her entirely, to the tips of her green toes, left her there. He was no more than twenty steps away when the rustling started, louder and louder, the whole tarp shaking as if by a growing wind; it was horrible to watch, horrible to listen to and angrier still he snatched it away, looked down at her closed eyes and the spiderweb in her ear. As he stood there her mouth opened very slowly, it seemed she would speak. He looked closer and saw a large white flower growing in her mouth, its stem wound around her tongue which moved, feebly, as she tried to talk.

He slapped her, once, very hard. It was disgusting to look at her, he wanted to smother her with the tarp, but he was afraid to try it again. He couldn't bear that sound again, that terrible rustling sound like the rattling of cockroaches, God if there was only some way to kill her fast he would do it, he would do it right now.

The white flower wiggled. Another slowly unfurled like a time-lapse photo, bigger than the first. Its petals were a richer white, heavy like satin. It brushed against her lower lip, and her mouth hung slightly open to accommodate its weight; it looked like she was pouting, a parody of a pout.

He threw the tarp away. He pulled down the blinds in the kitchen and refused to check on her after work. He tried to think, again, what to do, lay in bed at night hoping something would somehow do it for him. After a particularly heavy rain, during which he sat up all night, almost chuckling in the stern sound of the downpour, he rushed out first thing in the morning to see how she'd liked her little bath. He found her feet had completely disappeared into the grass, her hair gone into vines with leaves the size of fists, her open mouth a garden. She was lush with growth. He felt a sick and bitter disappointment, with childish spite wrenched one of the flowers from her mouth and ground it into the grass where her feet had been. Even as he stood there the grass crept a discernible distance forward.

Grass, all of it growing too high around her. Well when the grass gets too high you cut it, right, that's what you do, you cut it and he was laughing a little, it was simple. A simple idea and he started up the mower, it took a few tries but he started it. A left turn from the garage, walking past the driveway with a happy stride, pushing the mower before him, growling sound of the mower a comfort in his ears and all at once the ground trembled, was it the mower's vibration? It trembled again, harder this time, no earthquakes here, what the hell and it happened again, more strongly, over and over until the grass moved like water, choppy undulating waves that gained and climbed until he stumbled beneath their force and lost his footing entirely, fell down and saw with a shout of fear that the mower was still on, was growling at him now, the waves of grass aiming it towards him. He rolled away, a clumsy scramble to stand again, half-crawled to the safety of the still driveway. As soon as his feet left the grass the waves stopped. The mower's automatic cut-off shut it down. He was crying and couldn't help it.

"What do you want," screaming at her, tears on his lips, "what do you *want*," oh this is the last straw, this is enough. No more.

Back to the garage, looking for the weed killer, the ortho stuff he'd used before, herbicide, and the term struck him and he laughed, a hard barking laugh. He had trouble attaching the sprayer, the screw wouldn't catch and he struggled with it, the hastily mixed solution, too strong, splashing on his skin, stinging where it splashed. Finally in his heat he threw the sprayer down, the hell with it, he would just pour it on her, pour it all over her.

Walking fast across the grass, before she could catch on, before she could start up, hurrying and the solution jiggling and bubbling in the bottle. "Are you thirsty?" too loudly, "are you thirsty, Anne, are you—" and he threw it at her, bottle and all, as hard as he could. And stepped back, breathing dryly through his mouth, to watch.

At first nothing seemed to be happening; only her eyes, opening very wide, the eyes of someone surprised by great pain. Then on each spot where the solution had struck the foliage began not to wither but to blacken, not the color of death but an eerily sumptuous shade, and in one instant every flower in her mouth turned black, a fierce and luminous black and her eyes were black too, her lips, her hands black as slowly she separated herself from the fence, dragging half of it with her, rising to a shambling crouch and her tongue free and whipping like a snake as he turned, much too slowly, it was as if his disbelief impeded him, turning back to see in an instant's glance that black black tongue come crawling across the grass, and she behind it with a smile.

Bird Superior

IN THE INSTANT BEFORE the plane hit, he thought about the rabbit.

Ball of stumbling fur, right hind leg wrenched brisk and brutal, the stupid almost cartoon wideness of its eyes and he, swerving, trying not to hit it too. Again. Failing. The bloody fluff of its tail.

What a thing to think about, just before you die.

Cartoon character, him too, eyes as comically wide: Where am I? A hospital, that was obvious, less obvious the reason. What hurt? Nothing, so far as he could tell, but that could just be drugs. Unless he was dead and this was one of those out-of-body experiences. He seemed to be in his body, but how could you actually tell? He was in no shape to pinch himself. No mood, either, actually.

Emergency room. Not a central treatment area, a waiting room of some kind. Temporary storage? Maybe. If I can get someone to notice me, he thought, then I'll know I'm alive.

Green and baggy, white coat, stethoscope shine and cold brown hands, and his own timid voice: "Excuse me?" Am I alive? "Excuse me."

"Yes," businesslike friendly, not-impatient smile. "Mr., Mr. Kidler. John. How're you feeling, John?"

Alive, and with a vengeance. A name, even. "Fine," he said. "Am I hurt?"

"Well, you sustained a head injury, John, you've got some stitches in your scalp. Right across here," touching a numb line across, presumably, his head; he could see part of the gesture, but felt none of it. "Do you remember very much of what happened?"

"I remember," the rabbit. No. "The plane was in some kind of trouble, something about hydraulics?" Hopefully. Like a student, offering information to a notoriously exacting professor. Encouraging nod; it worked; he went on. "The flight attendants told us to assume crash positions, and we, and I did, and—" And what. Nothing. A small grayness, from there to here. The width of a scalp wound. "I'm afraid that's all I really remember."

"That's all right. It's pretty common," penlight in the eyes, were his pupils responding as pupils should? Blood pressure cuff. The gentle strobe of the stethoscope as the overhead light brightened, his own light above his own little movable bed. "It's a built-in safeguard, with this kind of accident trauma." Pause for pulse. "You'll remember when you're ready, probably within a week or two. Maybe more, maybe less. Different people react differently." Chart in hand, writing, absent nod of reassurance. "Nothing to worry about. Your main problem will be some discomfort in the area where the stitches are, but a couple aspirin every few hours should take care of that."

"Will I be going home soon?"

"We're going to keep you overnight, keep an eye on you. It's SOP for head injuries, nothing to be concerned about." Put the chart back, patting the metal U of the bed frame as if it were an extension of his body that could be soothed by touch. "If you have any problems, give a holler," and gone, and he left alone to trace, with clandestine embarrassed fingers, the line of stitches, his only evidence of cheated death.

An airline person came the next morning, he waking groggy and cold, his head and eyesight dull. Bright anxious smile, "How are you feeling today, Mr. Kidler?" For a minute he thought the woman was a nurse, until he saw, again, her blue suit, her chipper little tie. Nurses don't wear ties.

Chipper voice, too. He would of course be flown first class to his destination city—

"Detroit."

—as soon as he was ready to travel. Yes.

Not, note, "well enough" to travel. "What happened to the other people on the plane? Was anyone, was anyone hurt badly?"

No. No, thank goodness. Most of the passengers escaped serious injury, the plane itself sustained some structural damage; talking like a press release but obviously nervous enough to shit water. He took her card, let her go; exactly one hour later, another airline representative, this time definitely legal, was on the phone. This one was harder to get rid of but he managed, afterwards called the nurse, the real nurse, can I have an aspirin please?

Bitter dry taste in the back of his mouth. He slept most of the day, not drugged but simply tired, the body exhausted, maybe, by the furious inner work of healing; no one told him that but it made sense. The next day they told him he could go home. The airline said they were holding a first-class seat, they were sending an airline limo, would twelve-thirty be convenient?

"Twelve-thirty would be fine."

It was not until he was actually in line at the gate that he considered the concept of fear: fear of flying, to be specific, suggested to him by the mournful avidity of a fellow passenger, inevitably noting the Frankenstein panache of his stitches, his partially shaven head.

"Aren't you scared to fly, now?"

And he smiled, a dry modest little grin but there was actually nothing to it: fear of crashing, yes, perhaps a new appreciation of the force of gravity but he felt no apprehension at the idea of flying, felt in fact nothing at all. Perhaps if he could remember the crash itself things might be different, but things were things and he settled in his seat, buckled in, closed his eyes; he had done it a million times before. Though not, of course, in first class.

At work he was a minor celebrity; it wore off before the stitches came out, which was fine with him. What was the drama? A car wreck would have been worse. Certainly that roadkill rabbit thought so. Roadkill Rabbit, brought to you by Firestone Tires. If it had been a bird, now, it might have lived, able to take wing in the crucial second, able to find escape by rising. Pigeons did it all the time, blind nonchalant waddle before the oncoming wheels and just when it seemed inescapable, they rose, like swaggering preteens before an exasperated car: Let's see how close we can get.

He had begun to watch the pigeons, when he drove; they seemed to like roosting in underpasses, though you never saw them on side streets. Sparrows, on side streets, but they were a prudent group, skittish at the slightest sound of wheels. He liked to watch the incongruous seagulls, in from Lake St. Clair, stealing garbage from the dumpsters at the fast-food places where he sat eating lunch. Sometimes he saved the dry rind of his hamburger bun for them, maybe a couple of fries, the little ones nuked to near stucco consistency at the bottom of the container. The birds didn't care.

His head itched where the stitches had been, where the new hair grew; it wasn't growing in quite right, not coarse and grayish brown like before but downy. He frowned at it after showers, in mirrors, and then forgot about it.

Still he had no memory of the crash, though once he thought he dreamed of it: a smell like smoky plastic, the shrill staticky hum of the flight attendant's voice. The dream caused him no particular dread, left no larger residue of remembrance. He told his doctor about it. She was a big fat woman who didn't take shit from anyone and didn't believe in anything, including medicine.

"So what," she said. "Did it start your head hurting again? No? Then forget about it." She told him to take aspirin and if he kept having dreams, write them down and sell them to the movies. "Terror on Flight 505," she said. "One man's story."

In the mornings he heard the birds, not soft and sweet as he had always thought of birdsong, the idea of birdsong, but sharp, the efficient language of those without small talk. They woke him up too early but he didn't mind. He even considered getting a window feeder but was put off by the idea of bird shit stains on the side of the house.

All of this changed when he began to fly.

It was nothing he noticed right off, you don't wake up in the morning and decide you're going to fly, not even if you're the kind of person who has always dreamed of that quintessential freedom, which he was emphatically not: his dreams were more the hopeless Nobel variety, stunning some vast crowd with the fruit of his intellect, ha. At first he thought it was some sort of horrible delayed reaction, some insidious psychosis taken hallucinatory root: standing there in the cold morning driveway, bare feet an inch from the concrete as his lazy arms waved, what the hell am I doing? Two inches, three, his arms in perfect balance, his weight distributed and accounted for without the slightest thought, what the hell is wrong with me? Crazy. Crazy. He

stopped his arms moving and dropped lightly to the balls
of his feet, quick loping walk to the front door, stood trembling inside. He drove to work with the windows shut,
afraid somehow that he might pull over in traffic, attempt
to fly through the fumy air of rush hour, whee, look at me!

Birdsong, next morning, still completely incompre-
hensible and he was grateful, less so for the nagging sense
not of memory lost but of thoughts forever inaccessible,
profound changes made in those blank moments the fruit
of which he was only now experiencing, Ladies and Gen-
tlemen, I give you the Bird Man. Without thinking, absent
flapping in the shower, only noticing when the swirling
water, victim of a balky drain, did not lap as usual at his
ankles. Blowing his hair dry and a sudden suspicious peer
in the mirror, that downy patch, oh for God's sake don't say
it. Don't even say it out loud.

There was no idea in him to tell anyone, share this
delusion even to prove that that was all it was, frightening
enough the idea he might be going quietly posttraumati-
cally mad, but what if it were true? What if he were really
able to fly? By the power vested in me by a near fatal avia-
tion accident, I now pronounce you bird superior. Lift up
your wings and fly. Forget about it. Forget about it.

So much time spent in wasted nervous speculation, the
guilty staring out of windows at the shadows of circling
birds, work not so much suffering as, yes, grounded, the
simplest problems taking longer and longer to even com-
prehend, much less solve, the daily equation of life now
more riddle than plain sum and he asked for a long weekend and got it. Packed a gym bag and went up north.

The interstate visual white noise, landmarks he'd passed
so often he need never see them again to know his way. Styrofoam cup of coffee, some stale chips, he drove without

stopping. A campground, finally, he had been there many times, first with family, then buddies, and now standing by the hot hood of his car, finishing a well-deserved piss, the sun gone down and all the birds abed.

He slept in his car. No one there would check, it wasn't that kind of park. In the morning, the stale reek of the log cabin rest room, washing his face to the furious dawn accompaniment of a thousand birds or at least it seemed so, so many calling out at once. Barefoot, careful stride into the woods, surely it was too early for any watchers, bored or curious eyes, and he stood, suddenly sheepish, and as suddenly businesslike: right. You came all the way out here, now do it.

Rising.

Tremoring arms, nervous airless excitement mixed with a healthy horror of his apparently unconditional surrender to the strange but he was *doing* it, he really was. He was flying. Five, maybe fifteen, maybe eighteen feet off the ground, clumsy in the trees, sweat in his eyes and running down the wondering grooves of his gape. Wide-eyed. You bet.

The questions fell away with the ground below, there were maybe answers but he would never make it past maybe, so. His arms got tired more quickly than he had imagined, but of course it made its own sense, of course muscles tire. He wanted, bravado, to land on a branch but found himself unable to judge which might bear his weight, he was too far up to quibble so he chose instead the safer option of the ground, stood shivering with cooling sweat in the sudden shade of a tree whose topmost branches he had only just inspected, marveling suddenly on the true nature of perspective from a perspective that no one else could share.

Of course there was no chance of duplicating this stunt back home, in the neighborly confines of one-story houses and sensible streetlights, he must do all his aviating here and now. He rested awhile, hiked deeper, found a spot where he could see anyone coming—and why not, circling up in the green, the air so much different there in ways perhaps that, ground-bound, he could never have believed. He stayed up as long as his muscles dared, then, with bumbling exquisite caution found a branch, a lower branch than he wanted but one that looked substantial. And perched.

No one saw him, no birds approached him, that strenuous learning day, though he saw plenty of spoor, shit, and feathers enough to last a lifetime. He made his final approach at dusk, prudent in the last of the light, too hard to fly in the dark without radar. If he were a bat, now. You're an asshole, he told himself—perversely proud, rubbing aching biceps as he marched himself back to his car—asshole, that's what you are. He was too tired to drive, too sore to spend another night on the front seat. Back by the interstate there were motels, and he found one. Slept so hard he woke sweating, then slept again.

The weekend was all work, delightful, exhausting, it was amazing all there was to know, how in God's name did real birds do it? Instinct, of course, where he was learning the hard way, the hit-and-miss way, but then again he didn't have to eat grubs either. When he got into the car for the trip home he wondered, Could I make it, flying? Could I? No, reluctantly, the efficient gassy turnover of the engine, no, not enough stamina. Not yet.

And then shook his head at himself, amazed that one weekend could have sown such holes in his common sense, do you think you're invisible? Or don't you think a flying man is unusual enough to stop traffic, even on I-75? Asshole, he called himself again, less kindly now for he preferred his first reaction, he did not want to have to think in groundling terms. All the drive home he memorized the past days, the pure lack of not only care but the thought for care, perhaps the feeling was that it was all feeling, no thoughts beyond the physical, could it really be as simple as that? But if that were so, wouldn't, say, puberty then be holy, wouldn't the silent squeal of orgasm, the grunt and strain of a bowel movement, even though had cheaply, be just as pure? Was there nothing mystical to be had? nothing deeper than the sheer surface fact? Epiphany: love it or leave it.

It was hard, that night, to sleep in his own bed, he roiled the covers, the silent weary toll of the bedside digits making him more tired still but luring sleep no closer, and at last (he said) to calm himself he gave in: rose, a gentle stately indoor flight, once around the room and watch those turns. Mindful of the ceilings, of the frustrating low-bridge doors, he flew all around the house, twice. Arms alive, body soothed by the comfortable ache of muscles rehearsing newly learned tasks, he flew until his eyes would not stay open, then perched atop the metal storage cabinet in the laundry room, and fell to peaceful sleep.

Wake, early as is now usual, in some high spot: the fat overhead ledge of kitchen cupboards, the welcoming bookcase top. Eat breakfast, eggs over ironically, drive to work while playing placid the new game: distance calculated in air miles, how long would it take to get to, say, Atlanta from here? Phoenix? Seattle? How about Paris, you think you're ready for a transatlantic flight? He knew there were birds who did that very thing, flew unimaginable migratory distances, curlews or swallows or something; he didn't know the species, his new state of being had not led to any passion for ornithology. Imagine going back to Capistrano every year and being *glad* about it.

At lunch he continued his dumpster custom, finished the workday with a sense not of a job well done but a loan of time now completed for this day; fortunately he was a patient man. How much money would it take to live for a year, flying? Always assuming of course no capture, no eventual cage. This much? How long will it take to work for it? Very well.

And always at night the solo flights around the house, he was expert by now at avoiding lintels, ducking his head without having to think about it. Such a specialized ability, but no real need to be proud of it, birds did it all the time. All the time.

He still did not recall the plane crash, doubted now he ever would, certain that the memory was given in trade for what he had now, this elegant skill. Did it matter? certainly not, he had blundered somehow into far the better of the deal, had at times in fact a lurking feeling of unease: would it, somehow, be repossessed? And answered himself: Hopefully not while airborne, but knew in the calm secret silence of his mind that even if that were so he could not care or mourn it, what was living after all without this gift? the familiar pattern of the carpet beneath him, stained like a flight plan, the dust in unexpected places, his orbit was small but he cherished every inch of it. Once a month, the longer journeys, exquisite in their furtive challenge, building up those chest muscles, learning to taste the oncoming change of weather like a creature born to it; in no way was it reversion, he was definitely moving up.

What friends he had, at work, in the neighborhood, he had left behind almost from the start; there was no way to share this and there was nothing else he cared to share. He was pleasant, perhaps more distant than before but people notice less than we believe, their full attention a tithe not lightly paid, he discovered this fact early and traded on it in an absent way.

Mowing the grass, a casual wave, a morning pleasantry here and there, already so far away. The bank balance growing but not quickly enough; he sold some things, he would never need them now anyway, how much you want for that snow blower? Yeah? Leaf bagger for sale too? What're you up to, John, moving to Florida? His smile, pleasant smile and it said who me.

In the dark, up above the kitchen floor, seeing in memory to come the sweep of his arms, oars of flesh as he moved through the air, sizzle of the sun above much closer now, how wonderful it would be to fly at night, far safer but though he had considered it with obsessive care, even armed with his new expertise it was regrettably impossible, he simply did not have the eyesight for it and a light was out of the question: what's that, Earl? I don't know, but we better shoot it down. He had no intention of ending his flight in some back lot trophy's slump. Dawns, it would be, and careful, oh fanatically careful day flights, staying low and rural. He had even designed a backpack device, matchstick contraption of balsa and the thinnest synthetic silk, the kind hang gliders use: if absolutely caught and cornered he would give it to them, remember a show of vast reluctance, and then with luck escape. He was going to need luck no matter what, but it was not a dismaying observation, nor paradoxically gleeful: he neither sought or feared risk, he simply knew he would require some luck, would do what he could to make sure it wasn't much. It might be the ultimate in quixoticism, but he was still a practical man.

And then a night where, waking perhaps an hour before it was needful, he knew it was time, knew it with the thoughtless inarguable certainty of instinct, beyond sense common or uncommon. Down, readying himself, shower and food, a step beyond each action, a pace removed, excited not in any outward way but with a fierce good shiver at his core: did real birds feel this way the night before migration? Methodically but with slowly trembling hands he gathered all he would need, shut off the water, checked and locked the windows, strapped to his back the sly constructed fakery, its metal D rings (official looking unnecessary touch) the thinnest tinkling as he stepped onto the porch and locked the door. He even remembered to put in the mailbox the stamped letters requesting shutoff: phone, gas, electricity. The house was paid for, it would stand empty until he needed it, but to see it, illuminated by the cool swirl of headlights as he backed down the driveway, it seemed, felt deserted, abandoned as a nest lies empty; he would not be coming back there again.

It was a longer drive than perhaps was needed, but no matter what the end would be he would begin with caution, he would start off right. Leaving the car at the airport was, he thought, both clever and symbolic: obviously a planned departure, they would say, the man simply up and left.

Unusual for a metropolitan airport, it lay surrounded not by city but fields; besides the pimply cluster of Red Roof Inns and rent-a-car services there was little else but a smattering of faintly dumpy homes, not nearly enough together to be called neighborhoods, just blacktop throwbacks to a time when people preferred to live without noise. Birds probably felt the same way.

Dawn soon but not too soon, he could be, would be, well on his way by then. Hesitating, the insistent tremor already begun, clamor of muscles wanting to begin: still his eyes sought landmarks, still the nervous preflight shuffle, what was he waiting for? Faintly on the air the smell of jet fuel, remembering all at once a hard identical reek, some woman in the seat before him saying Jesus, Jesus and the unhappy shriek of something metal bending past all reasonable limits, his own balls trying to crawl up into his throat and if I could fly, this wouldn't be happening, no, not exactly so, not even close enough for paraphrase but it got him laughing and the laugh got him moving, rising, hard downward strokes and no man-made Icarus he rose, gained altitude, prudence far and away from the planes' heedless murderous thunder, skimming higher and higher, dark enough still for indulgent concealment, maybe a trifle self-indulgent but he was off on a great adventure, he owed a little to himself. Below him the sluggish glimmer of vehicles, still few at this time, were there rabbits running across that road? Too far, too high up to tell and that was anyway a problem for the ground, let those who lived there find an answer. No answers needed here for here there were no questions, between the glide of the clouds beneath him, and the bite of the windy stars.

Illusions in Relief

LITTLE BOY at the basement window, his grey tongue slack on the glass, small ugly face one big shiver of delight as Joseph, seeing him, rose, shivering himself, to readjust the makeshift paper curtain. Firm ripping noise of the duct tape no cover for the boy's sad grunt, his mother's snarl, curse and beseechment all in a word. Joseph's hand ached as he picked up the X-acto knife, silently slit one black-cheeked harlequin from the old magazine page on the table before him, added the harlequin to the larger distortion behind him: his latest work. It had brought the boy, and his mother; a fat white man with no hair and many boils; an old couple, ailment not casually apparent, who with the grim humor of wolves had stationed themselves just at the end of his driveway: we'll get you, sooner or later. They probably would, too.

Joseph dissected another harlequin, carefully poised its torso, doppelganger, beside the first—no. No, not there, steady fingers tremored just a little by someone's voice, not the boy's or his mother's but definitely one of the new ones, very close to the window.

"Please," just above his head, intimate and sick, "I want to *talk* to you, I only want to *talk* to you," as he placed the harlequin, studied it or tried to, "please talk to me, *talk* to me, *talk to me*," a groan, near-orgasmic entreaty, he imagined a mouth rubbing wide against the glass, drier than the boy's lips, scaly with a kind of saucy poison, the words it made unimportant beside the tone, the timber and reek of that voice and his hand was on the knife, he had cut and placed another piece without realizing: the first harlequin's head was now that of a lion, bald and nearly earless, eyes old with the limitless deceits of those promised to show it mercy; the second harlequin's torso issued, limp and smug, from the lion's bony mouth. The voice had stopped. Joseph set the knife down; he was very tired.

Upstairs, closed blinds, the unfresh smell of a house shut tight too long; if only he could open a window, one fucking window, was that too much to ask? Reaching for a beer he noticed with dull dismay that the refrigerator was almost empty, he would be forced to go shopping again. He hated shopping: they followed him around the grocery store, blocked his desperate cart with their empty ones. Hey, aren't you? I just want. Please, for my boy, my sister, my dad.

Can't shop, can't get gas, people following him home, inexplicably convinced of the help he could not give. Letters and notes and pictures, the pictures were the worst, jammed in the mailbox before they stole it. People rolling on the grass, digging it up—if he looked out there right now he was sure to see them, somebody was always digging up the grass. There was even a guy who was counting it; he wrote the day's tally on the sidewalk and threw a fit if anyone walked on it. Chipping pieces off the front porch, creeping around the backyard with lighted candles, leaving love offerings: food, porno magazines, obscure religious tracts. Once he had kicked open the back door, scattering them a moment, and "I'm not Jesus," he had screamed, "I can't help you, why don't you motherfuckers go home?" and that of course had only made it worse. No wonder the neighbors hated him.

Empty beer already. He opened another one, stood

drinking in the cool air of the open refrigerator, wishing he could get drunk and go to bed. Simple pleasures. No rest for the fucking wicked, though, or even the merely cursed. *God* they were fierce out there tonight, if he didn't get right back to work he was going to start seeing things and oh boy how he hated that. Oh boy oh boy. Snakes' heads in the shower, a face flying large around the kitchen, the severed limbs of blood-less fetuses lying scattered in the basement steps—*keep* your fucking brain tumors, your cancers and crotch rot and lost kids and lost minds, I'm losing mine too but there was no stopping, no, and he knew it, welcomed it too; he would not have stopped for the world, would not in fact have healed them if he could; ugly, selfish, true. He had never in his life done work like this and it was worth everything, all the waste and sorrow they shit on him, every holy dollop, every crusty squirt. Everything. And the pair of too-large eyes blinking solemn semaphore, just inches from his own, assured him with matchless conviction that this in fact was simply so.

He woke in his chair with a headache and wet pants: spilled beer, almost a canful, and he reached in angry ter-ror for the collage, had he spilled on it, fucked it up?

No. "God," he said, a soft statement of fact. It was even titled: *Working by the Light of Burning Human Bodies.* He turned on the gooseneck lamp to examine it more closely. "Jesus God," he said.

Nothing was waiting for him in the shower. He watched the *Today* show while he ate, the dregs of a box of Rice Krispies, all powder and grit. Somebody from a local talk show called. He didn't even bother to sneer at the message; his machine was full of them. Back downstairs to look, again, at the collage. Shivering, he turned it on the stack so it faced away from him.

It was always like this when a piece was finished: a kind of listlessness, a feeling of waiting for the next thing. Of course for sheer drastic grotesquerie he could always try a trip to the grocery store, in fact would have to and to hell with the cover of darkness, it never did him any good anyway.

It was always nerve-wracking, that first crack of the front door. Keys out and ready, face composed into a mask less indifference than sheer brick wall: go.

Heads, turning, and hands already out—more of them today, maybe thirty. Ignore them all. Somebody was rubbing at his calf, someone else grabbing for the sleeve of his jacket. He wrenched his arm away, kicked out his leg, small polka of revulsion, get *off* me and maybe he even said it out loud because somebody sighed, somebody else said please and oh Jesus it was the magic word, pleasepleaseplease like a swarm of insects. He slammed the car door without even wondering if hands were there. Screw them. Something else he couldn't cure.

He spent the ride home worrying about the money he had spent. Very soon he would have to choose between food and the gas bill, and after that, what? The house? Stop it, he told himself, maybe it won't come to that, maybe it'll stop and they'll go away. Yeah, and maybe one day they'll break in and *eat* you, oh boy, and he had to laugh at that.

He knew with a dry certainty that he could have sold the collages. Anybody crazy enough to camp out in his backyard for weeks on end would surely be crazy enough to pay large sums of money for what they thought was a cure. He would sooner burn them, every one. Bad enough that this inexorable craziness had rushed into his home, his very life, worse yet that his reactions to the visions their sickness sent had gone beyond merely shaping to dominate his work; he would not commit the final act. A voyeur, yes, without trying but it was still the truth. But he was not a whore. They sent things to him, he made art from them, a closed loop and that was that, final.

Halfway down the street, almost home when he saw with despairing clarity that the crowd had doubled at least; word was out, then, that the hermit had emerged. Now he would have to fight his way in, with groceries yet. Rage made his head pound, he felt like running them over, all of them, human bowling pins, whee! Stop it, he said, you're crazier than they are, but the image would not leave him and he had to laugh. Welcome to nirvana.

As it was he could only manage two bags. Investigating the contents he was depressed to find SOS pads, tomato sauce, pepper, and paper towels, a hearty ragout, you bet. "Son of a *bitch*," and back he went, get the rest or die trying.

He was halfway up the porch again, grim elbow-out death march, when a woman in a red jogging suit fastened on him and would not, would *not*, let go. He was actually dragging her along and she was no lightweight, he was losing breath, slowing down when out of the bubble of faces sharp muddy-brown eyes, no rapture there, meeting his and all at once the woman let out a mighty howl and dropped from him, yelling "He punched me in the *tit!*" and in the sudden grateful lightness Joseph gained the door and slammed inside, sagged to the floor with the bags and laughing in breathless bursts.

The cold of the basement, why was it always so damp, what the hell was he doing down here anyway. Half-asleep, and in the corner of his midnight bedroom some dog, graceful bas-relief ballet, paws hanging broken and the bones of its throat hideously warped, warping still under an incredible inner pressure until the head blew free like geysering water, hounding him, ha ha, all the way down the stairs, whispering half-heard prophecy until he threw an empty bottle at it just to shut it up.

The bottle shattered on the wall, glass sparkling across the sheaf of collages; he sat down, sighing, to work. Was working. Had been, how long, who knew. Assembled before him a picture of a scalpel, of a little girl, of a fat woman masturbating, of a bottle of 1890's patent medicine, Never Fails to Bring Relief. I've heard that about a lot of things, he thought, and started to cry, a dull monotonous sound, huh-huh-huh like air squeezed in bursts from his chest, heard above the noise his name. Someone saying his name.

[Joseph]

Who was out there tonight, looking brown-eyed at the house, at him, standing bareheaded and serene in the dark, a warm peculiar itching on a forearm, just above the ancient mottled wrist.

[Joseph let me in]

"Fuck you," he whispered, "fuck you to death," warm snot on his lips, too sick to wipe it away, too tired. Nothing is worth this, nothing.

[Joseph]

The back door curtains, pinned shut for your protection, the porch light hadn't worked since he bought the house. Opening the door, no tears but still that endless chuffing sound, he stared out at the diehards, a part of him remarking Shit you look even crazier than they do, and an old man, brittle and fine as an antique weapon, scratching at his arm as he stepped up to the door like a step in a dance, raising one forearm and the sleeve of one forearm to display with silent assurance—surely this will interest you—an irregular coin-shaped patch, the skin a rich and deadly green.

"Joseph," the same voice in and out of his head, and he grabbed the old man by the other arm and dragged him in.

"Cures anything," the old man said, lifting his beer.

"Cheers," Joseph said. He was possessed of a marvelous lightness, a full and expansive drunkenness that was less a state than a symptom; he felt better than he had for months. "Who're you," drinking, "Santa Claus?" and he laughed again; it seemed he had done nothing but laugh since the old man came in.

"Who gives a shit what my name is." The old man drank again, let out a thin scentless belch. "Watch this," and up with the sleeve again, poured a few drops of beer on the green spot. Joseph leaned forward to see the beer foam up like raw acid, sink back into the skin. The spot. The old man looked at his face and laughed.

"I knew you'd like it."

"I can't," leaning back, far back, "I can't do anything about that."

"Oh yes you can."

"I said I can't fix that."

"Who wants it fixed?"

Morning, Joseph waking to a half-stale cooking smell and bounding up, in terror that he had somehow left something on the stove, was the house burning, or—Ah. Memory. The old man sat at the kitchen table, eating the last of a piece of wheat toast.

"You sure got a shitload of food," he said.

"I buy in bulk." There was coffee. Joseph sat across from the old man, who promptly hauled up his sleeve: the green spot had easily doubled. "Just being in the house helps," he said to Joseph.

Joseph rubbed at his face. "Things are getting too weird even for me."

"Don't start," said the old man impatiently. He took a beer from the refrigerator. "We went through all this last night."

"I don't remember that. I don't even know why I let you in." He didn't either.

The old man stared at him over the rim of the can, slow slide of Adam's apple in the veiny tube of throat: not unhappy, or hysterical, or worshipful or greedy, not wanting.

"Everybody gets what they don't want," he said. "The trick is to find a way to want it. But that's not your problem, is it?"

Joseph said nothing.

"Your problem is, and stop me if I'm wrong (but I'm not): you don't want to go where it wants to take you. Like me. But I got over that. All I want now," tapping his arm, "is for this to go on."

"And you want me to help you."

"I want you to work. You get where you're going the way you're meant to get there. If you don't jerk yourself off with a lot of shit about guilt. Save your own fucking soul, you know?"

"Jesus. Philosophy."

"Jesus is philosophy." The old man finished off the beer, hollow aluminum thump on the tabletop. "Let's go."

Joseph thought he would feel like an asshole, did as he sat down, supremely conscious of the old man, like a column, behind him. Turning green. "Fucking *A*," Joseph said, and started in again on the dog collage. Scalpel and little girl, fat woman, the patent medicine dripping, running, long voluptuous stream like a waterfall, infinite relief, infinite cure, peace is flowing like a river. His busy hands warm at the palms, cool the tips of his fingers. Sweat on his back. Yes. The little girl, daisy-faced and hair a river too, the fat woman's come a river, the scalpel splitting skin to make the biggest river of all and all of it winding into a road leading into darkest peace, a vortex not black but green, a deep wet green.

Joseph raised his head, smiling, took a long happy breath and saw the old man move, just a little to the left; he had taken of his shirt and was staring as happily at his arm, which was green to the shoulder.

"Just look!" the old man said, and waved his arm like a trophy, then bent to examine the collage. "Pretty good," he said. "Better than anything those other fucks ever sent you."

That night they had an amazing drunk, all the beer in the house, watching the greening of the old man. Joseph told him everything, everything that had happened since the first time, that original supplicant, his first vision or dream: "I thought I was going crazy," Joseph said.

"I bet you did." The old man drank. "I bet you were."

"I called the police," shaking his head, tired amazement still at his own naivete. "They told me I'd have to press charges, you know, for trespass. OK. Fine, for the first one or two. Or ten. But after that, shit." Slow sluice of Pabst Blue Ribbon. "They tried to make out it was my own fault, attractive nuisance, like I had too many Christmas lights or something. The traffic was *incredible,*" and incredibly he laughed, and the old man laughed too. It *was* funny in a way. A weird way.

"Open another one of those for me," the old man said.

"You got it." Snap pop off comes the top, drink it on down and we'll never stop. He told the old man about the reporters, tabloids, and minicams, the failed attempts to make it stranger than it was which had to fail because there was no way, no *way* it could be: the shared hysteria of ten, twenty, fifty people, faces changing all the time, chasing their terrified messiah who wanted only to be left alone.

"Pictures," he told the old man bitterly. "Of babies. With no arms. Pictures of old people with big fucking tumors, *close-ups* of tumors. Dead wives or missing kids or who the hell knows what. They taped 'em to the window. Facing in. That was when I used to try to open the drapes." More beer. "*Why*, you know? Why do they think I can help them? It wasn't me made them crazy." And the visions, more certain with each one that he was going madder, working under their pernicious influence and waking to find grotesquerie, and beauty, beyond anything he had ever hoped to do: a power so harsh he was helpless before his own talent, magnified by their need, by the pain they carried like the seeds of some rich disease. Manna in reverse. The multitude feeding him.

"How can I say no to it?" wild, spilling his beer, head pointed to the ceiling, compass of grief revealed. "I don't want them to be hurt, but I can't help them anyway, and they keep *giving* me this stuff, how can I turn it down? How can I do that? I can't do that."

The old man opened another beer for them both, drank with lips green at the corners. "Come on," a gentle hand on Joseph's. "Back to work."

Waking to darkness. The old man, long swath of color in the metal folding chair. Joseph had to piss something terrible. On his way back from the bathroom he chanced a look outside: they were still there.

"Hey," second day, third? Who knew. He had done six new pieces. "Hey. What the hell's happening to you anyway?"

The old man's luminous smile; his teeth were as falsely

white as ever. "Feels great," he said. "Riding the current usually does."

Eighteen, nineteen new pieces, they poured out of him like water. The old man was totally green now but insisted there was more to come, wait, just wait a little longer.

"Wait for what," said Joseph, but mildly. He felt better, oh God how much better he felt. He hadn't had a vision, a hallucination, since the old man came, except of course (of course) for the ones the old man carried, but those, oh those were different. Because they actually did something. For someone else, someone besides Joseph. Although they left him with an aftertaste, a restlessness that was perhaps a curve in the circle begun by the old man, instigated by the offering of his willful mutation, a cycle that nourished them and itself: more art equals more change equals more art, infinite cure, yes. Never Fails to Bring Relief.

The people outside did not leave but no new ones came. Joseph, pointing at the collages, told the old man, "Then these must all be for you."

"Not really," he said.

Palms to cheeks, a long yawn, Joseph rubbed his eyes to consider this last piece: the pristine alien beauty of wasps in promenade, long black streamers like cries of wonder from the skeleton children beneath, skeleton mothers askip in their own inimitable waltz. He turned, to display it to the old man, hey look at this.

"Hey, look at this," he said, turning all the way in his chair. Nothing. "Hey," louder. He got up, still holding the collage, walked all around the basement. He realized he didn't even know the old man's name. He went upstairs, searched the house, collage in hand, "Hey!"

The front door was unlocked.

He sat in the chair nearest the door to consider this. The collage was still in his hand. Someone knocked at the door and he opened it. It was a girl, young girl, with a mild case of acne and no right hand.

"Here," he said, and gave her the collage. As it left his hand and touched hers one of his fingers blossomed a bright and ineffable green.

Reckoning

DREW HAD BEEN DRIVING for most of the day, most of the week if you counted the stop at Lucy's parents' house, and it was raining, and he was tired. Slap and shiver, slap and shiver, the monotonous beat of the shredding wiper blades was driving him crazy, even over the radio he could hear it. In a burst of petty rage he pounded the switch to off, but that was worse, like looking through a shower curtain, and then he had to laugh: stop at the next place, he told himself, whatever it is, stop at it.

Shirlee's. Big crooked lettering, homemade sign nailed up over the previous owner's more professional effort, but it didn't matter, it was a place and he was stopping. Ankling through the puddles, into a smell of frying, coffee strong but not fresh, a weak frost of steam on the street fronting windows. Two customers and a waitress sat talking; she moved with reluctance, palming up her little green order pad when it was apparent Drew was sitting down to stay.

"Hi," Drew said, trying for sincerity, stopping when he saw she didn't care either. "Can I get a breakfast or something?"

"You can get anything you want we got." They negotiated, and she came back with coffee. Setting down the cup she said, "Little late for breakfast," and Drew shrugged. Breakfast had always been his favorite meal, and he ate it whenever he could.

God, what a drive. The coffee's heat showed him how sleepy he was, and he rubbed his dry eyes, looking out to the lessening rain and the careless way he'd parked. Fuckin' wiper blade. Have to get it fixed. If Lucy—Shut up, he advised himself, and breakfast came and for awhile he could.

Full, he was even more tired. Driving on was out of the question: he could never make Robin's place tonight. He debated finding a motel, but he had already spent most of Elliot's check and every day's gas made him broker. So. Sleep in the car.

Paying, he asked the waitress whether she knew the whereabouts of a liquor store. Disdainful directions, but he was used to that, and with a twelve pack cold on the seat beside him he went hunting for a parking place, somewhere where no one would holler trespass or call cops who'd tell him to move along and bust him if he couldn't. Shitass little town like this, it would be harder than it looked; a million places to flop in the naked city but here every inch was sacred to somebody, he would have to cruise awhile.

It was past dark, finally, when he came to rest beside a long dirt road, gravel-pocked like acne and leading not only from nowhere to nowhere but so nowhere in itself that there were no tire marks save his in the wet. On the left, twenty-thirty feet back, was a house and something, garage, shed, out back, but it was so obviously abandoned that it took only a second to decide to pull up behind it, stash the car and his sleeping self where it was doubly safe. The grass and weeds were garden-lush there, deep, dripping, long wands bending as he stepped through them to take a piss, hoping his passing would scare up nothing bigger than a chigger.

Back in the car he popped a beer and risked the radio, but it was either droning gospel or twang and neither was worth running the battery down. He didn't care, though, for silence; there were too many thoughts in silence, and too many of them were of Lucy.

Shut *up,* but this time it wasn't working, and she came back, gray-hazel eyes and small breasts like peaches, big unselfconscious toothy smile that came less and less as things went worse. She could love and she could fight, and of the two she was a better fighter; far better than he, especially in the downhill days: coming home from her job at the hospital and him on the sofa, drinking beer and watching Bugs Bunny on channel 31, sketches and odd twists of clay in the discard pile on the floor, and her purse slamming down and open, plastic circle of lipstick rolling out as hands on hips she shouted she was tired of it, of his lazy ways and his lazy face and if only God'd made her an artist instead of an RN what she couldn't do with it, not like *him,* nothing but a waste. Sometimes he could ice her back, sometimes laugh her back, but towards the end (The End) it had gotten very tough to do either, and in one acrimonious burst he had gone off, stayed away for half a week—and miraculously, he had laughed when it happened, chuckling over the sheer timing of it: a commission and a big one, big for him anyway, some tin-ear band with money to blow blowing it his way. He had taken their down payment, drunk only ten bucks of it (and four of them were Robin's) and swaggered home, shiteating grin and all, meaning to *show* her, both ways.

No lights on, her car gone; she was showing *him,* then. Well. He could wait. He passed the time sketching, fiddling with the band's existing logo, doodling till the phone rang: MaryLee down at the hospital, and had he heard.

They all thought he was drunk at the funeral, even Robin; only, oddly, Lucy's parents knew different, knew his shouts and staggers were the product not of booze but hysteria, grief cranked to where he couldn't hold it, where it filled and mastered him and smothered what sense he had left. He cried like a slob right there at the grave, wet face pressed into Mrs. Dooley's shoulder, and she rubbed his back like he was her own, her living child. Afterwards Mr. Dooley took them both out for brunch, and Drew ate three bites of eggs over easy and threw up all over the men's room floor.

Eight months, and still he could taste those eggs. The beer was cold, it made his fillings ache and that was good. He killed the can, tidy toss into the backseat, sat head back against the window and feet on the seat, staring half at the fabric-peeling ceiling and half out into the dark, where the empty house sat like camouflage, its dark green paint weathered and scabbed to vegetation, its windows so dirty no sunlight could betray them to a vandal's stone. "Coulda been a nice house," he said, popping another can. "Coulda been another Tara. As God is my witness, I'll never be thirsty again." This beer was as cold as its twin, but tastier; the second one usually was.

By the third he was almost asleep, would have been but for a pressing need to piss. Groaning, muscles bitching, just drunk enough not to care he was barefoot in all that knee-high green, he stepped away from the car, peed in a long luxurious stream, eyes half-closed. If you stood away from the trees, you could see the stars, very clear tonight despite the earlier rain or maybe because of it. He squinted, mourning lost knowledge: he used to be able to name all the constellations, twelve-year-old finger pointing confident authority at the vastness up above. Now he was lucky if he could find the Little Dipper.

Hand on the door, bending to step inside, and a flash, a silver shine like a baby star but much much lower, on his level in fact: by the garage, shed, whatever. Someone was there.

"Shit*fire*," underbreath anxiety, thinking Don't get your hair up till you know what's what, wishing he hadn't had that third beer, wishing he could put his hand to his big-barreled flashlight in the messy maze of the backseat. He had to look away to find the flashlight and when he did peripherals told him the light had flashed again, and this time there were two lights, not one.

Well. He had nothing to steal but the rest of Elliot's check, and, of course, the Chevy, the beer too if they wanted it. It would be bad to be ripped off and stranded but it would be worse to have the shit kicked out of him and maybe more, so if it looked like a smart idea he was going to pretend he couldn't find his glasses and couldn't see fuckall without them, couldn't see if the robbers were crazy teenagers or men from Mars. And first he was going to wait and see what was what, and do it in the car if possible.

Shine again, much closer, and a definite shape: a woman's shape, surprise surprise. White, *white* skin, and tall; couldn't see hair or face but she was shiteating poor if what she had to wear was all she had, poor enough to really live there, poor enough to gladly play decoy to a stranger if she could get enough out of it to buy a new pair of jeans. Her walk was easy, not tense in the dark, a confident twist to her head like this was Buckingham Palace and she was maybe gonna call out the guards if he couldn't come up with a good reason to be double parked. And still the shine: was she wearing mirror shades or what? and where was the light that made them shine?

"Hey," a voice as self-assured as her walk, low voice, actressy. "Got car trouble or something?"

"Got no trouble, ma'am," trying for easy, coming up short. "Didn't know there was anybody—"

Up to the car now, up where he could get a good look at her face, a real good look. Not shades, no.

Eyes.

Silver *eyes,* silver fuckin' eyes like a fish's scales, no whites, no irises, no nothing but silver, and his hand was reaching on its own for the ignition when her hand, smarter than his, slipped out the keys.

"Calm down," smiling, he could see her smiling. God her skin was white. Maybe she was some weird kind of mutant albino or something? Men from Mars, ha ha, Lucy used to say how God heard even the things you didn't say out loud, *especially* the things you didn't say out loud, oh Lucy please go away I have to *think.*

And then he knew he was *really* going crazy, because Lucy was there, too. Really there, not just one of his ten-beer figments, there enough to get a whiff of her: dry cinnamon odor, ragged T-shirt, standing behind the other with a smile half-happy, half-something else, her eyes as silver as the chrome on his Chevy. Saying, "Hello, Drew," putting out her hand, reaching to draw him out of the car.

"Fuck a *duck,*" he said between his teeth, mouth full of loose sour spit, scrambling to roll up the window as the first woman reached in and put both hands on his face. Her hands felt surprisingly good, coolish, soft-palmed, the nails long but not too long, holding his face, gentling his clenched jaw, thumbs just brushing his cheekbones while enormous darkness blew down like a summer storm, darkness entire, the Lucy smell very close indeed and he thought Crazy *and* dead, *God* what a night.

It was still night when the darkness cleared, but he was out of the car, crosslegged on a bare floor, linoleum, a pattern like Woolworth roses and sick pansies. His jeans were wet; apparently death had been unnerving enough to make him piss himself. Lucy sat across from him, hopeful smile on her face, the other woman to her left, and to her left three others: a man and two women.

"Feel better now?" Lucy said, so completely Lucy that, dead or no, he began to cry: long steady ribbons of water, his hands clasped between his trembling knees, weeping to see her there, wearing not the pale prim dress she'd worn in the coffin but a Braves T-shirt and a pair of men's cutoffs, cinched around her tiny waist with part of a bicycle tire tube. He cried for that tire, cried to see her here in this crummy place, cried to be here in this crummy place. She didn't make thirty and neither did I, he thought, and cried harder for a minute, then calmed a little.

"Hey," he said, "hey, Luce," and she came to him, sat head on his shoulder like she used to, and he spoke not to her but to the other, his tone mild yet still somehow aggrieved, as if he was owed at the least an answer.

"Why'd you kill me for anyway?"

She laughed, a genuine sound, and after a second the others did too, all but Lucy. "I didn't kill you," she said. "You're not dead."

That stilled him, put a long chill on his skin; the flesh of him that touched Lucy pulled back a little, just a touch. "Then how'm I here? How—"

"They used to call it a glamour," she said. "It's a way—" Shrugged, sighed, impatient with the need to explain. "It's just a way to get your attention."

"Well, you got it." He looked down, head cocked, at Lucy. "Are—" A hard question to ask, and the other knew it, spoke it for him, still with that impatient edge.

"We're all dead," nodding to Lucy, the others. "Me, Lucy, all of us." The man nodded, a ponderous motion like he'd needed half the day to think it up; he hadn't been any Einstein when he was alive, that was sure. The other two women nodded too, both dressed in ragged red, with red bows in their hair, bows made from dusty Christmas ribbon it looked like. A mother-daughter act probably. They didn't really look alike but then kinfolks didn't always.

"Listen," Drew said, straightening, his body still wanting to pull away a little now that it knew it was still alive. He leaned forward, part of him wondering, in a distant musing way, what was keeping him from making one assbusting dash for the door, the same part deciding it must be, what, the glamour or whatever, "listen, I would just like to know a few things, I would like to just ask a couple—"

"Lucy can tell you all that," the woman said, standing suddenly, brushing back that long black hair; and it was *long*, and looked clean even though she didn't. "I'll talk to you later on," and turning away, as if bored, beckoning to the others, mother-daughter getting up at once, daughter with a definite Charley McCarthy lurch, and the brain surgeon last of all, cradling in his big hands what looked like a jar full of dirt. They went into the room adjoining, no one looking back, and at once Drew heard them talking, not about him, nothing even scary, just the kind of aimless talk you talk with a roommate or coworker. Stone crazy now, he thought, and the thought did not displease him, nor did Lucy as she smiled, that big happy billboard smile, he hadn't seen it in so long. "C'mere," she said, though he was still next to her, "c'mere, you," and suddenly she was *there* in yet another way, the self of her, the body of her, and he was holding her very very close, not crying now but feeling as if he might, a big clean sob to blow away that day by the grave and the taste of eggs and all the days after, all the time spent pushing her memory back and never succeeding. He did cry after all, and she held him, almost exactly as her mother had eight months before. Her hands were gentle, and he reached to hug her back, stroke and soothe as she stroked and soothed, but then his hands wanted something different, wanted it now, and his breath was sudden and ragged, panting on her cool white neck, fingers dragging at the soft tatter of her T-shirt, bending to her lips to find them closed to him, smiling but still closed, her kiss loving and warmer than her skin but her breath, then, not sour but arid, dry like driest wine, a puff of it against his cheek as with her palms she guided his head lower, put her breast to his lips which opened at once, her nipples like little cherries, sweet as her mouth was not. The bicycle tire snapped in his hands, the cutoffs fell from her bony boy's hips, he yanked his own jeans open and was on her, in her, the linoleum dusty-cold against his palms, the pleasure immediate and so fierce it stunned him, sunk him to lie atop her, unable to catch his breath, and she smiling as she always had, the gentler version of the billboard, saying, "Just rest now, baby, just rest," and he though that was a wonderful idea, he had so much to say, ask, but he would say and ask it in a minute, just a minute, just let him get his breath.

His back was sore as hell in the morning, and he thought Man this seat is *hard* until he woke enough to see the Woolworth roses and the sun weak through filthy windows, and a great surge of adrenalin threw him standing and halfway out of the room, heart astammer and throat rich with the taste of vomit. The door, the door, where the hell is the fuckin' door but there in the doorway Lucy, smiling, not looking any different except of course for her new style in eyeballs, saying "I got some stuff from out of the car, if you're hungry."

"God," taking deep breaths, willing the terror away. She looked so *normal*, little paler than usual but put a pair of Ray-Bans on her and she could pass for living anyday—

"Lucy," actress voice, behind Lucy, "did you talk at all to Drew last night?"

Lucy shrugged, smiled. The other shrugged too, a different way. "Well, somebody has to talk to him, there's things he has to know. And it better be pretty quick, because he's not looking too cheerful this morning." Brisk, almost pissed, "You want the short form, Drew? While Lucy gets you something to drink?"

"Beer," he heard himself say, a croak like his voice was changing. "In the car."

Lucy nodded, not pleased with her role as waitress, a look between her and the other as she left the room, Drew staring down at his feet until the warm can touched his fingers. He sat down, hard, popped and drank half the can in two long swallows, gave a short spasmodic belch and drank the rest, more slowly. "OK," he said when he was finished. "OK."

Lucy sat beside him, the other across from them both. "I said short form, right," she said, producing from somewhere a pack of cigarettes and a scratched red lighter. The smoke came out silver from her mouth, and Drew flinched, hard. She grinned, blew more smoke. "Pretty, isn't it? I used to spend *days* doing that. —Anyway. You want to know what's up, right? Well, I can answer your questions."

"You sound," Drew said without thinking, "like a social studies teacher I had once. Miz Minch. Minch the Pinch."

She laughed then; she had a beautiful laugh, like a waterfall, not loud but very clear. "OK, OK. Drink your beer and shut up. Lucy, you fill in anything I forget, OK?"

Her name, she said, was Norah. She had "been here" for almost a year, after her death. She came up out of the ground.

"Fuck."

"Yeah, I know, but it's not as bad as it sounds." Her skin had been that glossy white, her eyes silver: all physical evidence of her death was completely gone. "I had a messy end," she said, with such bitterness that even Lucy looked away. She had come up ("come up," Drew thought, the beer threatening to do the same) in the little field behind the house, naked, mute, in a walking coma of terror. She came into the house and found Edie and Darleen, the mother-daughter act only they weren't really related, had never known each other "before." "Wesley either," naming the large silent man. "Wesley came the week after I did." Norah frowned. Wesley was a suicide, she said, hung himself in his basement rec room after his wife decamped to Nashville with his brother. "Wesley came out somewhere by the interstate," Lucy added, the way someone else might say Wesley is from Pittsburgh. What had led him to the abandoned green house, scent or instinct or chance, no one knew. Wesley himself was deeply uncommunicative, preferring to pass the time by entombing insects in Peter Pan jars packed to the top with dirt, then watching the jars to see if bugs, too, could "come up." Wesley was obviously seriously strange, but Norah said that seemed to be the way with a suicide: Wesley was the least normal, the most dangerous, the only one who still showed scars. "You can see his rope burns if you look," Lucy said, "but don't look."

"Don't worry." He popped the second beer. His hands were shaking.

"Edie and Darleen are from somewhere else too, but they won't say where." Norah sighed. "Edie's all right, but Darleen's not what you'd call all there. I don't think she ever was, really. Death intensifies the characteristics you had in life, and if you were a mess then you're a bigger one now. The—the process of coming up is," long pause, "kind of traumatic. It could probably fuck you up big time if you weren't pretty stable to begin with. Like the suicides. Who are probably *very* disappointed when they figure out what's up. —Anyway Darleen bought it in a car wreck, her boyfriend was drunk, but if he died, too, he didn't come up anywhere she could see, or maybe he did and left her. She tells it both ways. Edie died of cancer and came up behind the 7-Eleven."

Drew laughed, a big nervous bray that once out could not be stopped. He laughed so hard his hands stopped shaking, kept chuckling even as he nodded for Norah to go on. "I'm sorry," he said. "I really am. It just—I don't know, it just struck me funny."

"Right. Well, you know what happened to Lucy." That stopped him; doubtless she had known it would. "We saw her walking around one night, she was like sleepwalking, and we brought her in here. Since she came, we haven't seen anyone else. Until you."

Dubious: "Nobody?"

"Couple scares, but nobody really got close enough to know what they were seeing. I glamoured one of 'em off, this old drunk guy. Drove away and that was it."

She went on, through the second beer and half a bag of Cheetos (both offered to them, but no, they didn't eat or drink, thank you). They did not, could not, roam far—it was much too dangerous, one slip and that was it, and though Norah was unsure if they could die again she was in no rush to find out: "Once," with that great bitterness again, "was quite enough."

"You mean to say you all've been here, since, ever since—"

"Ever since we got here." Lucy's smile was somber. "Not much in the way of entertainment, but then again nobody's tried to burn us as witches either."

They were obviously not witches, not vampires or zombies or even that good old standby, aliens—Drew's own knowledge of Lucy had proved that to him—"but these," Norah's long fingers resting beneath her eyes, "these would take a *lot* of explaining."

"Angel eyes," Lucy said, half to herself.

"That's what Darleen calls them." Angel eyes could see, but better, they could *show:* their pasts, though nothing between death and coming up; present lives, theirs and others'; sometimes, "maybe," Norah's voice half-skeptic, "the future. But not like prophecy."

"That's your opinion," Lucy said at once. This was obviously some kind of bone between them; Drew knew that look when Lucy wore it. "*I* think—"

"What we know," cutting her off, "ain't much. From what we can prove, the future stuff is all jumbled, garbled, like flipping channels too fast. Like runes, or oracle-talk. Hard to figure out, and harder to believe."

"Bullshit," said Lucy promptly. "What about when Darleen's sister—"

"I wouldn't exactly call that prophecy, Lucy, but if you—"

"Wait a minute, wait a minute." Drew waved his beer can, head aching worse than his back. "I don't know what the hell you guys are talking about."

Norah, abrupt: "Would you like to show him?" and Lucy, just as sharp: "*Fine,*" then swiveling to Drew, taking a breath, and her eyes came alive.

Still silver but in the background, and the scenes she chose convinced him: their last fight, her shouts, his shouts, the Lucy in her eyes yelling "If only God'd made me an artist instead of an RN" and all the rest of it. He didn't cry; almost, but last night had cried him out. Instead he was wretched and looked it. When the scene was through, he squeezed his own eyes shut and said, in a voice too low to be heard without straining, "I am so sorry, Luce."

"Babe." Fondly, rubbing his shoulder; she had meant, some, to punish, and in succeeding could be gracious. "Forget it, it's over now, we're back together. I just did that one because I knew you'd remember it real good, enough to catch all the details. I can do a lot of other ones, too. Everything I remember, and even some things I didn't remember till I did 'em. Do you remember once we went to Six Flags with Marsh and MaryLee and—"

"Thing is," Norah, hands on knees, her own eyes aswirl with pictures too fluid to decipher, "nobody can figure out why we can do this, or what it means that we can. Lucy thinks we can prophesy, too. I don't, but I don't know for sure, either, and we can show some version of the future. What all this has to do with coming up, and why funeral homes aren't busy putting in revolving doors, I don't know and neither does anyone else."

"Or," Lucy, looking thoughtful, "why we don't come up where we went down."

"Right. All we know is what we've learned from each other in the time we've been together. And it's not enough. We don't even know if there are other people like us."

Drew rubbed his forehead. God what a headache. The smell of the house was worse in daylight, ancient slat board stink and the dry reek of dust and old mildew, crawling up the walls. A spider strolled past his foot and he crushed it at once, grinding it into the linoleum with childish violence. "Why don't you use your angel eyes to find out? If you can see the present, like you say, then you should be able to look around and see if—"

"We tried," Lucy said. "Didn't work."

"Well why haven't you tried a little recon on your own? What about doing what you did to me, that glamour or whatever?"

"Too short-term." Norah, long brows together, teeth bending a thumbnail. Her skin looked even whiter than Lucy's; maybe it was the black, black hair. "Believe me, I've thought of all the avenues. Lots of time for contemplation, you know," lovely bitter face, turning away. "All the time in the world."

A silence, lasting too long, the smell of the house suddenly too much and he stood, uncomfortable, saying, "I gotta take a leak." Out to breathe sunny air, deep breaths like relief, like coming up from the catacombs. Coming up, ugh. From the corner of his eye he could see Wesley, amateur entomologist, conducting another of his experiments in metaphysics, crouched with the peanut butter jar a holy inch from his face. Drew passed him carefully without speaking. Do not disturb.

They were arguing, Norah and Lucy, arguing over him: Lucy's voice scaling to the high C of anger, oh did he know that voice, and Norah's voice deeper and more vehement: "—set up housekeeping?"

"I don't see where it's any of your damn business."

"What you're afraid of is that once he takes off he'll never be back."

"And what are you afraid of, Norah? Huh? What scares you?"

As he walked in the argument stopped; not ended, stopped, both sets of shining eyes turning towards him, tracking him as he moved. They both seemed to be waiting for him to speak up then and there, make one win and one lose. "Listen," he said, conscious more than ever of his body, the sheer physical weariness, the aches and the pains, things they obviously no longer considered or cared to, "listen, I am just really worn out, you know? I've been driving all this whole last week and I gotta be somewhere in the next couple days." To Lucy's narrowed gaze: "I'm supposed to be at Robin's by the end of the week." Her gaze narrowed even further; Robin had always topped her shit list. "Listen," suddenly angry, "I never asked for any of this shit, you know it?" Silence. "And I have a commission, this guy in Florida, he—" Fleeting unhappy thought of how little money he would have after Jim Elliot's check was gone. God what a mess all this was. He would have to think about it, think a way through, but right now he was tired, too tired to do anything but sleep. Saying nothing else he passed them, out again to his car, where he rolled down all the windows and clipped his keychain to a belt loop, no one was going to be taking any unscheduled drives, no, uh-uh, and before the next thought his eyes had closed, he was asleep.

He woke to heat, early afternoon, his legs cramped but his headache gone. He was hungry, thirsty for something other than warm beer, and after finger-combing his hair and changing T-shirts to one a half-shade cleaner (its block-lettered motto, "To Think Is to Act, Only You Don't Have to Stand Up," seeming peculiarly apropos) he backed out and away, the engine shockingly loud in the heat and empty quiet, the smell of growth and wild decay. Hair and eyes at the window, Norah watching him go, as silent as the landscape.

The town was even drearier in daylight than in nightfall's rain, garish 7-Eleven and frowzy Frostee Boy, fat-bellied mothers and kids with faces clowned with the day's playtime dirt, a laundromat, Shirlee's, Best Bros. Funeral Home (shiver of hilarity, all present and accounted for?), a gas station. He bypassed the liquor store, double backed to the more crowded 7-Eleven where he thought there was less chance of being recognized. Buying the things he needed, enough for two maybe three days, he was grateful no one remarked on his presence; he felt exposed, conspicuous, the stranger in town. What if someone followed him, just to see, just for something to do? Like those two boys there, big boys, sitting smoking in their panel-rusted pickup, watching him. Were they watching him?

He drove well within the speed limit, heading in the opposite direction for five, eight, thirteen miles, sweating every time a car came up behind. The gas gauge said a quarter of a tank, enough to get him to the house, and maybe to a gas station in the next town, wherever that was—he damn well wasn't going back *there* again. Ugly nowhere place.

At the house he angled into the same spot, thought better of it and pulled up even closer, hiding place. He sat on the hood to drink his Pepsi, sweat on his upper lip, on his back, under his arms. Lucy came out to sit beside him, shading her eyes from the glare off the bumper, and he felt like laughing.

"Got what you needed?" He nodded. "Drew, what're you gonna—"

"Right now I'm gonna drink this Pepsi, if that's OK with you." He rubbed the coolness of the can against his lips. One of Lucy's hands fingerwalked down his thigh, up again, down again.

"I know this is hard for you," she said.

He switched the can to his other hand, put his arm around her. "I missed you," he said.

She kissed him. He kissed her back, the can leaving his hand to roll, red and shiny blue, into the long sweep of grass, like sinking to the bottom of a pool. She kissed him harder and he led her back into the car, onto the front seat, arms trembling as he lowered himself atop her, the smell of her in his mouth, her hair in his eyes.

Then after, rubbing his back, not complaining though his weight pressed her down and she had always disliked that (maybe it didn't bother her anymore?). "What're you going to do, Drew?" A voice softer, somehow, than before, but with an edge to it as foreign as her eyes. "Are you gonna stay?"

"Luce, I have things I—"

"Selfish as usual," gunpowder temper with a faster flashpoint, "and please get off me, you're crushin' my stomach."

She slid out from under him in one neat pretty motion, pulled T-shirt on and sat glaring. "Lucy," leaning forward, "I wish you would just understand that—"

"I understand that you were out drinking with Robin Butterman while I was dying," and that was the end of that conversation.

He sat alone in the baking car, fished another can of Pepsi from the back. She had died and he had not, and there was no way to make that equation equal, no way to atone for the sin of outliving her. No matter what happened, what he did or didn't, her death would always be there, big black grand slam on the scoreboard, casting its shadow before her like a scepter for a queen. "Shitfire," leveling himself free of the greenhouse front seat, hunting the dashboard for the sunglasses that were sometimes there.

Norah sat on the ruin of the front porch, looking at the road and the trees, smoking. Long plume of silver smoke, her head arched back like a fire-eater's, eyes closing in the sun. Her throat was as white and pure as a porcelain vase. When he sat beside her she silently offered him a cigarette. He had stopped smoking two years before; he lit up like a condemned man.

"This is all too weird for me," he said, almost apologetic, looking as she did toward the road. Something, some bug, rose high above the grass, shimmered like a dragonfly before it swooped away.

"Speaking of weird, how'd you like the town?" and when

Drew rolled his eyes she laughed. "Yeah, they're bigger freaks than we'll ever be." She made a smoke ring, watched its perfect dazzle fade on the brightening breeze. "Do you know, when I first came here, I used to sit out here with a pocketknife, a little green pocketknife, and cut my finger," demonstrating, imaginary blade biting left forefinger, "just like that, over and over again. It was just like a mouth, you know? The cut I mean. And I would do it over and over, just to watch the little mouth open and close." She laughed again. "You should see your face. Lucy caught me at it once and yelled her head off. She was scared. I scared her."

You scare me too, he thought, but didn't say it. She dropped the cigarette, ground it out with her heel. Her bare heel. "I don't like it here," she said, and went into the house.

Lucy came to him again, but not until night, late, her skin like milk and snow in the strong moonlight, her blunt little fingers digging into his back. But her heart wasn't in it, and she left him soon after, not angry but somehow sad, and far away. She had bound her hair into a little pigtail, and it made him want all at once to cry. He wished she had something better to wear than those fucking cutoffs. He should give her his clothes, something. He opened a beer but the first swallow almost gagged him. He stood, reached to scale the can into the darkness, then thought better of it and poured it out, yellow gurgle between his bare feet, warm and flat as piss. Pepsi or nothing, then.

Of course tomorrow, or the day after, there would be no more Pepsi, no more Oreos, no more twisted strings of beef jerky like mummy's fingers (God what a thought, no more beef jerky for him), nothing at all to eat, and he was damn sure not going back into town. Maybe there was something in the next town, maybe a McDonald's where he could use the bathroom, get a wash. He had to be pretty rank by now.

"The dead have no noses," he said aloud, deep fake anchor-man voice, and cracked up, head back against the seat, his laugh winding down like an engine's sighing stall. He had to do something and pretty quick, too. Maybe find a phone, call Robin, and—what? Not explain, no, but say something. What? Dunno, but by now Robin must be starting to wonder; Drew had never been punctual but he had never before failed to show up. Would Robin start making phone calls, asking around? Would he call the Dooleys? (God what *about* the Dooleys? Should he tell them about Lucy? *Fuck.*) And what about Jim Elliot and his advance check? (Which would soon be history. Don't think about it.) There was work to do, money accepted, wasn't it fraud to keep money when you had no intention of doing the work? It was some kind of stealing, anyway, and if Jim Elliot thought he, Drew, was ripping him off, he was in a position to do something about it. Gee, Mr. Elliot, I guess I lost track of the time, I met up with my dead girlfriend and we got to talking, you know how it is.

Hot breeze dwindling to no breeze, cold-looking stars up overhead, what a fuckin' mess he was in and no mistake. A big shape moved before him, startling him into fear, and it took an overdrive moment before he knew it for Wesley, which was still pretty scary so he went inside. No sign of Norah, or Lucy, just Edie and Darleen, alone in the empty house. Edie was brushing and braiding Darleen's hair and telling her the story of Rapunzel, her voice the gentle monotone one uses to soothe a cranky child; Darleen, somewhere in her twenties when she took that last joyride, was obviously loving both the story and the hairdressing; her eyes were closed, and from his unobtrusive post by the door Drew could almost hear her blissful purr. He watched for awhile, saying nothing, listening to the story with half an ear, when suddenly Darleen's eyes popped open like shades rattling to, and in them a jerky scene of himself, going, leaving. She wasn't smiling, and Edie wasn't either, so he took the hint and left them there, mother and daughter, alone in the dark. Storytime.

Restless, he went outside again, circling wide around the big bug-hunting figure in the outer yard, sticking to the spaces between house and, what, shed? garage? Whatever it was it was just this side of falling down. He couldn't see the stars now, the green overhead was too dark, midnight green like the paint on the shed, long blisters that he peeled with his absent fingers to show the rotting wood beneath. He thought he heard voices, imagined them Norah's and Lucy's, but then they stilled and he heard nothing, nothing but the bending grass of Wesley's passing, nothing but the circle of the stars.

Not yet light, but coming to it, and he did hear voices now: their voices, Lucy's very high and tight, Norah's clipped, biting off each word like teeth through crackling tinfoil. They were close by the car, very close, by sitting up even a little he could see them: leaning into each other's faces, if they were men they would be punching by now and in fact Lucy was raising her hand, and he held his breath, but then she dropped it, turned, abrupt fluid graceful stomp away. Towards the field, while Norah's stomp took her towards the house and him. "What the hell're *you* looking at?" she snarled, pausing by the car door. "Never seen a cat fight before?"

Stay cool, he told himself, don't make it worse. "You guys woke me up," small neutral shrug. "Couldn't help hearing."

"Well then I suppose you heard your girlfriend's plan, such as it is. If it were me, I think I might object to a honeymoon here on hell's little acre, but maybe you think that's a fine idea." She lit up a cigarette, tiny fire flare showing pictures in her eyes, fast forward, much too much to see. "You know it's funny," mean-eyed, blowing smoke in his face, silver cloud, "she hates your guts for leaving her, but she—"

"I didn't leave her! I just, I wasn't there but I *never*—"

"Personally," cutting him off, shutting him down, "I don't give a shit. I know you're not about to start a talent search on my say-so, but she thinks you're going to run off first chance you get."

"Well what if I did?" Riled now himself, voice getting louder, argument range. He imagined the others listening. Let 'em. "What if you all did? What's keeping you here anyway?"

"I'll tell you something," leaning into him, hair swinging, eyes too fast and she knew it and slowed down, standing still so he could get a good look. Looking: and he saw her, sick, sick in bed, puking blood on green sheets and white floor, two people, parents, sitting on visitors' chairs, blood on her mother's cheap nylons and Norah saying "I got fucked in more ways than one." It came like a chant, the first words of a strange strange song and he realized that she was crying: beautiful, shocking, strands long and silver, not like water but tinsel; tears from angel eyes fragile as angel's breath, more tears as the pictures changed, every fear, every bad thing that ever happened, ever could happen in a hospital, every bad thing that had happened to her in the terrible course of her illness, all of it magnified into a grotesquerie greater even than its fact. Shadow on her face like clouds before the moon and her voice, low and rageful, "One good look at me, all it would take is once and then a cage in some kind of *hospital*, put me away you bet I'm fuckin' scared because I won't I will never *ever* EVER GO BACK TO THAT!" screaming, the tears something else now, squirming lines, twisting in the dirt as she screamed even louder, then stopped as if her throat was cut and he heard it too, then: feet on the gravel road, a man's voice, not Wesley's, a voice just crossed over to manhood and eager to prove it. "C'mon this way," it carried like a shout and Norah grabbed his arm, sharp nails digging in, rushing him through the tall grass, weeds whispering around his legs.

He didn't think about Lucy. It shamed him when he finally did, crouched breathless behind a pile of John Deere junk and rusting paint cans in the shed, rat shit between his toes. Norah's eyes shone, then stopped; she had sunglasses, his old sunglasses, capping the beacon, hiding what a flashlight might find. His heart was beating so hard he thought he might faint, fall over, throw up; his hands were colder than hers.

"I seen one of 'em," oh my God how close they were, he could hear them through the broken window, "big one runnin' off across the field. We can get that one later, if you want," and a second and third voice deciding, speculating, "Well I just don't want—" and a shriek, high, not Lucy, Edie maybe or Darleen, and the voices outside the window broke into shouts and ran, heading for the house.

Norah's lips against his ear, hoarse: "Past the field there's trees, can you climb?" and her voice was so small he could hardly hear it, hardly believe that the other, the sentry, had, hardly had time to think before he was knocking things over to run, run, fullbore onto something sharp and he grunted at the pain in his foot, it hurt so bad he had, he just had to slow up, Norah ahead like a ghost, a vanishing point of light, spirit guide. He dropped to one knee, had he cut off his fucking foot or what, and then the sound before the pain: boom. A little boom. And then a very big pain, so big as to dwarf the one in his foot, so big as to steal his breath. He fell right over from his one-kneed crouch, on his back in the weeds, staring at the stars and feeling, somehow, as if he could not move without instructions.

They came, finally. Four men, just past being boys. The littlest one carried the rifle, and it was his voice that cried, "Oh shit this one's normal, this one's just a guy!" and he wanted to tell them it hardly mattered because this one was pretty close to being worm chow anyway. God this had turned out to be a real kinghell mess, now hadn't it; if only things would stop hurting. The boys were gone. Had Norah gotten away? Lucy. Oh Luce I am really just so fucking sorry, I guess you were right before, I never am there when you need me. God this hurts. A bug, walking across his face, tiny tickling questing feet and he wanted to say, Look out for Wesley, but there really just was no air, no air left. Vacuum, and dark coming down as the sun came up. Like, like a glamour.

"Cold down there," he said to himself, "cold, *cold* down there." It was all he could think to say. He pushed, but his arms were weak, the muscles stretched and tired as if he'd spent the night slinging pianos. Pushed again. Like giving birth, and that made him laugh, he had to laugh at that. Pretty bright for nighttime: he could see every hair on his arms, see the dance of the blood beneath his white skin.

The ground seemed to suck at him, dirt in his nose and dirt in his toes and dirt up his tired ass, but he was persistent, that was all it took, sticking to the job till it was done. "Cold up here too," he mumbled when he was free, sat beside the tunnel his body had made to wipe the dirt away as best he could. Being naked didn't help either: he saw the goose bumps rise, flash flood of them, and that was kind of funny too, but this time he lay back to laugh, to rest. Such a pretty moon tonight, all silver, bright as a quarter, as a shiny eye. "Bring some clothes," he said aloud, "bring some clothes when you come," and closed his angel eyes.

The Company of Storms

LIKE FALLING INTO THE SKY, the lake was so
smooth with stars; only the faintest tickle of surf, the
most minimal sigh. Northward the private beach, long pale
playground for the expensive summer homes that stood
above, designer concoctions colored like false driftwood.
Here, below the two-by-four boardwalk, built last summer,
decaying creosote tang and already begun splintering
against the fringe of beach grass pruned dry and wicked at
the ankles, the slender slope of iron-dusted sand, its damp
black powder swirled to strange confectionery patterns in
the greater width of ivory-brown: this was public land. Pop
cans and beer bottles, remnants of cheap fireworks, the
sticky skin of used condoms, the mysterious shape of half a
toy: a half-submerged tide of detritus grown from the cheap
seeds of an afternoon's entertainment, abruptly thinning as
it passed the makeshift sign onto private land, as if the sand
itself respected the artificial division of wealth.

Past midnight, almost one, in a darkness still lush with
heat. A heavy red sign advised that the beach closed at ten
PM. But the water is always there.

In the parking lot, softly grinding over gravel, a big dark
blue Chevy pickup with a heavy-duty winch. Its lights were
off. Behind it a Dodge van, its color the combination of
road dirt and burnished Bondo, back doors roped shut
with a messy length of heavy coated wire. The pickup rode
a careful half-circle around the edge of the boardwalk,

onto the beach itself, the tread of its passing a crude mosaic in the sand. The van stayed where it was, motor idling, from its interior the bass heavy distortion of a cheap stereo turned too loud. The side panel door slewed open, faint descending tinkle of empty cans. Somebody said, "Shit," and then, "Help me pick these up."

No one answered. Four people began walking towards the beach finishing off the last of their beers, as the pickup turned in slow pirouette to face the water. Seventeen, eighteen, no older, elaborately shushing each other like noisy kids pretending to be quiet in class. The one left behind turned off the van's engine, making the silence seem larger than it was.

"Whose turn is it?" said one of the girls: louder than the rest, brassy, with the kind of top-heavy allure that sours early. In one sloppy swallow she drank off her beer, let the can fall. Her question brought shrugs, the desultory small talk of disagreement. The boy in the van had finished picking up the beer cans and was now walking towards the group. The wind seemed to rise a little. The boy who had driven the pickup, a tall boy with shabby cutoffs and stork legs said, "I went last time."

"Then it's your turn," the loud girl said to the boy nearest her, blond and heavy-shouldered, as if he played sports, football maybe, or lifted in the gym. He had one arm around a thick-waisted girl in a Beach Bum T-shirt, with long hair that blew in pretty tangles around her face. "If you're so hot about it, Sherry," she said to the loud girl, "why don't you go?"

"That's a good idea," said the other boy from the van, voice deeper but not too deep, not as deep as the lake or the darkness, not old enough to be too deep. He poked her in the upper arm. "Why don't you take a turn this time."

"Fuck you, Griff," she said. "You know I can't swim that good."

"Then just float on your boobs." General laughter, Sherry's pantomime slap, the low arch of the moon behind a drift of carbon cloud.

"It's Griff's turn," said the boy who had turned off the van, now close enough to guess the conversation. "Rob, me, Dan, Griff." He nodded at the sky. "We better get going. It's gonna rain."

"It's not gonna rain, asshole," but Griff began to move towards the water, a freshening stroll that ended with his half-comic dive into waist-deep darkness, disturbing the austere patterns of star on water. The rest stood watching. He stood, blowing water, swinging his hair to throw off the excess. The blond boy hollered, "You chummed up good?" and he waved an arm to say Yes, OK, then dove again, resurfacing to call, "Better get the truck ready," and down again.

The stork-legged boy hopped into the pickup, circled it so it was winch-side-in, the back tires brushed every so often by the rising kiss of the water. "Go on," the blond boy said to Lewis. "Get the van."

They watched him lope back to the parking lot, hopping quick and painful on some small booby trap, broken glass maybe. The girl named Sherry snickered. The blond boy said, "You think he'll ever find out about his dog?"

His girlfriend shook her head. "That was mean," she said. "Poor Petey." Sherry snickered again.

"Oh for God's sake," she said. "The dog was twenty years old or something, it was gonna die anyway. Besides, if it wasn't for Petey, we'd've never found those things."

"It was mean," the other girl repeated.

"Hey, the dog's the one that went after the fucking thing—"

"*You* threw the Frisbee right *at*—"

"Man's best friend," the blond boy said, in an easy tone, "let's forget it. Is there any more beer?"

The van, moving like a tired old dog, rolled in slow idle down to the water's edge. Lewis leaned from the window, checking his proximity, checking down the private side of the beach. Nothing, not even the glitter of beach fires. He flicked the headlights on to shine in patterns on the fractal waves. In the water, Griff waved once as the lights came on.

The blond boy opened a can of beer and he and his girl-friend began to pass it back and forth. "I wonder what that guy uses them for," she said.

"Who knows. Just be glad he does." The blond boy wiped his mouth on his arm.

"He probably chops 'em up for bait or something," Sherry said. "Or, you know, dissects them. For science."

"Science, shit," the blond boy said. "He probably sells 'em to freak shows, those alligator farm things they got down south. Griff's uncle said he met him at the fair, right? At the sideshow."

"So?"

"So he sells 'em down south or something." His girl-friend, grown bored with the conversation, lifted her lips; they kissed, a long kiss; he rubbed her breast through the T-shirt.

Lewis looked away, towards the diminishing stars, muted as if in denial of the conversation, as if saving up the lightning for later use.

"Maybe medical research," the stork-legged boy said. "You know: cut 'em up and see how they work."

Sherry made as if to snatch the beer from the blond boy, who evaded her with an easy backstep. "I bet you're right," she said. "I bet it's for a carnival or something. 'See the Sea Monster! Wonders of the Deep!' Like a freak show," growing more animated, "in a tank, you know, and people can go up and touch the glass."

"Fun," the blond boy said. His girlfriend shifted closer to him; almost absently he squeezed one cheek of her ass. Lewis said, "They can drink lightning."

"What?"

"Who can?"

Nodding out past the swimming shape of Griff, to the larger darkness beyond. "Them." No one spoke. "You can watch them," Lewis said. His voice was peculiar, almost too soft for his insistence. "From right here where we are. They stand up, they rise up through the water and they—"

"Oh bullshit," said the blond boy scornfully. "Nothing can—hey. Hey, I think he's gettin' one! Look," and they all moved a little closer to the water, Sherry wading in to her calves, her knees, the blond boy and his girlfriend close behind her. Lewis stayed farthest behind, sand crusted small on his ankles, the tops of his feet, sweat on his back through the skin of his T-shirt.

In the water they could see the extravagant gusts of foam, far higher than any wave tonight could warrant. The stork-legged boy backed the pickup a careful foot closer, then checked the chain on the winch.

"Get ready!" The blond boy's voice had risen with his excitement; he sounded younger now. "I think he's coming in."

"Big one," Sherry said. Stepping backwards, she almost tripped; Lewis reached to steady her but with negligent avoidance she shook off his touch. In the showy yellow of the pickup's headlights the stork-legged boy and the blond freed up the winch's chain, unclasping first the heavy hook that bound the loop. The stork-legged boy hopped back into the pickup. The splashing was loud now, strangely rhythmic; they could see, along with Griff, another form. Big. Sherry gave a little whoop, backing up all the way to where the other girl stood beside the van. The wind had risen; the girls' hair blew freely, like streamers at a fair, flags before the freak show. The blond boy gestured with the looped chain to Lewis, like a cowboy with a lariat. "Help me here," he said.

Together they waded out into the water, closer to the gusting, the artificial bursts of foam. They could see the strong pinwheel of Griff's arms, the heavy wake behind. "Careful," said the blond boy, wading slowly so he did not splash. "He's a big fucker." In silence they moved on an intersecting line, each increment tolled by sand, the irregular nip of pebbles; the water slapped at their upper thighs in rising rhythm, faster as the foam rose, the startled waves ascended, faster as Griff and the darkness that trailed him grew closer and closer, the girls' small cries and Lewis's sweaty hands on his half of the chain, keeping it steady, holding it tight with the blond boy as the water splashed them to the waist now, higher, the stroking rhythm reaching them at last in a churning freshet of sound and stink and confusion, Lewis's cry and Griff's yell and the blond boy's airless grunt, swinging the chain, heavy chain, swinging it hard. And again. And again, the blond boy almost crying for breath, bending to the whorl of water and swinging once more with a last shattering strength to find, at the end of the chain, quiet. And a dribble like oil on the water, some strange slick rainbow of fluid unseen but felt, with the dabbling fingers, with the itching skin of the thighs.

They stood, the three of them, in the abrupt and welcome quiet, the slowing waves; something heavy beneath the water, unmoving, bounded by the circle their bodies made. Panting like warriors, Griff with one hand to his side.

"Fuckin' stitch," he croaked. "I almost—" A sigh, and no more talk for a moment; they could hear the girls' voices but none of their words.

"Didn't I say he was a big one?" The blond boy peering down. Lewis closed his eyes. From the beach the girls called questions. "Stupid," Griff said. "Somebody'll hear."

They bent in purpose, hands working in a rhythm undiscussed, cinching the looped chain around the chest of their quarry, binding it tight. The sky above had lost much of its stars, instead showed the deep bland blankness of an incoming storm. "It's going to rain," the blond boy said. "Let's get this thing in the van."

He waved, to give the sign to the stork-legged boy. The oily sound of the winch, starting up, the strain of metal: hard, to haul this massy weight, drag it through the resisting water, as if the lake itself was unwilling to see it gone. Separately beside it the boys moved in, keeping an eye on the chain, making sure its reel was smooth, its burden safe. When they reached the beach, the girls had the van doors already open.

"Lift it up," Sherry said.

Slippery ripple of uncertain light on heavy green flesh, lagoon-green and scales, a salty, oily smell like sardines. Or the sea. The body was easily eight feet long, invested with an almost balletic delicacy about the feet; hands? Part of the scales were missing on the low ridging slope of forehead, a smeary tear, left by the chain, in the flesh there. A ruff as fragile as courtier's lace rose behind the damaged head, moving feebly in an unconscious, respirationlike rhythm. The eyes did not open but moved beneath the lids, restlessly as a child in a fever, in a disturbing dream. The four limbs were slack, the heavy truncated tail limp against the sand. The chest moved, once, and the ruff shivered, as if in some strange physiological sympathy. Watching, Lewis felt his own chest ache, and turned away as if shamed, turned back to face the dark starless water and the slowly cloaking stars.

Sherry touched it with one extended toe, on its silent breast; then jerked back, giggling a little too hard.

"It's cold," she said.

"It's supposed to be cold," the stork-legged boy said. "It's a lizard."

"Do you think," said the other girl curiously, "it could be a kind of dinosaur?"

"I'll tell you what I think," her boyfriend said. "I think we better get it in the truck, that's what I think. Griff, man, help me with this a minute."

Together they unlooped the circling knot, unwrapped the chain; slowly the winch drew it back. With the quiet grunting of real exertion, the four boys were able to load the resistless body into the empty van; it fit well, like a piece in a puzzle: even the tail proved malleable. The stork-legged boy carefully closed the van doors, as carefully tied them shut with the red coated wire.

He nodded at Griff. "Followed you pretty good back there. Were you scared?"

"Shit yes," Griff said, and they laughed, all but Lewis. "The fucker must weigh four hundred pounds."

"Four hundred pounds," Sherry said, "four hundred dollars." She sounded drunker now. "That guy isn't gonna be there all night," she said. "Are you guys ready or what?"

The stars were invisible now, sheathed by the heavy clouds. Insects moved in the brisk lunatic circles of agitation, smelling the storm, their ballet backlit by headlights, by the faint sizzle of the makeshift light above the boardwalk's parking lot stairway.

The stork-legged boy revved the pickup engine. "Who's

ridin' with who?" he asked, and Sherry immediately climbed beside him, slamming the door too hard. The blond, his girlfriend, and Griff were already in the van.

"Lewis," the blond said. "Hey. You driving or what?"

"You drive," Lewis said. "I'm gonna walk back."

The pickup pulled away, taillights bright and gone. "It's going to rain any minute," the blond's girlfriend said warningly.

"You go on," Lewis said. "Thanks anyway." He watched them leave the parking lot, turn left; it was a twenty-minute drive out to the warehouse.

He walked back down to the water, scuffing gently at the sand. His arms ached from exertion, hurt where the chain's friction had abraded. He sat on the very lip of the sand, where the water could touch him, where he could dip a finger if he chose, or choose instead to swim entire, as far as breath could take him, up or down as was his whim. Out towards the horizon there were the sharp new flickers of the rising storm, still too far to hear their thunder. He thought of a long green body, rising up as if in the grip of some pure epiphany, head thrown back to the long impossible white. Drinking the lightning.

The temperature dropped by five abrupt degrees. If he strained, he could hear the thunder now.

Deep rustle of the long beach grass, insects' last desertion and the faintest incongruity, smell of salt then swept to nothing by the incoming wind. It grew colder still, too cold to stand before the waves, growing waves rising rough and clean to smooth by their presence churned depths, sand runed by thrashing, by motion, by a cold green body, by disappearances large and small. When at last the storm broke the beach lay innocent before it, docile and empty as the eyes of a sculpted child.

Teratisms

"**B**EAUMONT." Dreamy, Alex's voice. Sitting in the circle of the heat, curtains drawn in the living room: laddered magenta scenes of birds and dripping trees. "Delcambre. Thibodaux." Slow-drying dribble like rusty water on the bathroom floor. "Abbeville," car door slam, "Chinchuba," screen door slam. Triumphant through its echo, "Baton Rouge!"

Tense hoarse holler almost childish with rage: "Will you shut the fuck *up?*"

From the kitchen, woman's voice, Randle's voice, drawl like cooling blood: "Mitch's home."

"You're damn right Mitch is home." Flat slap of his unread newspaper against the cracked laminate of the kitchen table, the whole set from the Goodwill for thirty dollars. None of the chairs matched. Randle sat in the canebottomed one, leg swinging back and forth, shapely metronome, making sure the ragged gape of her tank top gave Mitch a good look. Fanning herself with four slow fingers.

"Bad day, big brother?"

Too tired to sit, propping himself jackknife against the counter. "They're all bad, Francey."

"Mmmm, forgetful. My name's Randle now."

"Doesn't matter what your name is, you're still a bitch."

Soft as dust, from the living room: "De Quincy. Longville." Tenderly, "Bewelcome."

Mitch's sigh. "Numbnuts in there still at it?"

"All day."

Another sigh, he bent to prowl the squat refrigerator, let the door fall shut. Half-angry again, "There's nothing in here to eat, Fran—Randle."

"So what?"

"So what'd you eat?"

More than a laugh, bubbling under. "I don't think you really want to know." Deliberately exposing half a breast, palm lolling beneath like a sideshow, like a street corner card trick. Presto. "Big brother."

His third sigh, lips closed in decision. "I don't need this," passing close to the wall, warding the barest brush against her, her legs in the chair as deliberate, a sluttish spraddle but all of it understood: an old, unfunny family joke; like calling names; nicknames.

The door slamming, out as in, and in the settling silence of departure: "Is he gone?"

Stiff back, Randle rubbing too hard the itchy tickle of sweat. Pushing at the table to move the chair away. "You heard the car yourself, Alex. You know he's gone."

Pause, then plaintive, "Come sit with me." Sweet; but there are nicknames and nicknames, jokes and jokes; a million ways to say I love you. Through the raddled arch into the living room, Randle's back tighter still, into the smell, and Alex's voice, bright.

"Let's talk," he said.

Mitch, so much later, pausing at the screenless front door, and on the porch Randle's cigarette, drawing lines in the dark like a child with a sparkler.

"Took your time," she said.

Defensively, "It's not that late."

"I know what time it is."

He sat down, not beside her but close enough to speak softly and be heard. "You got another cigarette?"

She took the pack from somewhere, flipped it listless to his lap. "Keep 'em. They're yours anyway."

He lit his cigarette with gold foil matches, Judy's Drop-In. An impulse, shaming, to do as he used to, light a match and hold it to her fingertips to see how long it took to blister. No wonder she hated him. "Do you hate me?"

"Not as much as I hate him." He could feel her motion, half a headshake. "Do you know what he did?"

"The cities."

"Besides the cities." He did not see her fingers, startled twitch as he felt the pack of cigarettes leave the balance of his thigh. "He was down by the grocery store, the dumpster. Playing. It took me almost an hour just to talk him home." A black sigh. "He's getting worse."

"You keep saying that."

"It keeps being true, Mitch, whether you want to think so or not. Something really bad's going to happen if we don't get him—"

"Get him what?" Sour. No, bitter. "A doctor? A *shrink?* How about a one-way ticket back to Shitsburg so he—"

"Fine, that's fine. But when the cops come knocking I'll let you answer the door," and her quick feet bare on the step, into the house. Tense unconscious rise of his shoulders: Don't slam the door. Don't wake him up.

Mitch slept, weak brittle doze in the kitchen, head pillowed on the Yellow Pages. Movement, the practiced calm of desire. Stealth, until denouement, a waking startle to Alex's soft growls and tweaks of laughter, his giggle and spit. All over the floor. All over the floor and his hands, oh God Alex your *hands*—

Showing them off the way a child would, elbows turned, palms up. Showing them in the jittery bug-light of the kitchen in the last half-hour before morning, Mitch bent almost at the waist, then sinking back, nausea subsiding but unbanished before the immensity, the drip and stutter, there was some on his mouth too. His chin, Mitch had to look away from what was stuck there.

"Go on," he said. "Go get your sister."

And waited there, eyes closed, hands spread like a medium on the Yellow Pages. While Alex woke his sister. While Randle used the washcloth. Again.

Oxbow lakes. Flat country. Randle sleeping in the backseat, curled and curiously hot, her skin ablush with sweat in the sweet cool air. Big creamy Buick with all the windows open. Mitch was driving, slim black sunglasses like a cop in a movie, while Alex sat playing beside him. Old wrapping paper today, folding in his fingers, disappearing between his palms. Always paper. Newsprint ink under his nails. Glossy foilwrap from some party, caught between the laces of his sneakers. Or tied there. Randle might have done that, it was her style. Grim droll jokery. Despite himself he looked behind, into the backseat, into the stare of her open eyes, so asphalt blank that for one second fear rose like a giant waiting to be born and he thought, Oh no, oh not her too.

Beside him Alex made a playful sound.

Randle's gaze snapped true into her real smile; bared her teeth in burlesque before she rolled over, pleased.

"Fucking bitch," with dry relief. With feeling.

Alex said, "I'm hungry."

Mitch saw he had begun to eat the paper. "We'll find a drive-through somewhere," he said and for a moment dreamed of flinging the wheel sideways, of fast and greasy death. Let someone else clean up for a change.

There was a McDonald's coming up, garish beside the blacktop; he got into the right lane just a little too fast. "Randle," coldly, "put your shirt on."

Chasing the end of the drive-through line, lunchtime and busy and suddenly Alex was out of the car, leaned smiling through the window to say "I want to eat inside." And gone, trotting across the parking lot, birthday paper forgotten on the seat beside.

"Oh God," Mitch craning, tracking his progress, "go after him, Randle," and Randle's snarl, the bright slap of her sandals as she ran. Parking, he considered driving off. Alone. Leaving them there. Don't you ever leave them, swear me. You have to swear me, Michie. Had she ever really said that? Squeezed out a promise like a dry log of shit? I hope there is a hell, he thought, turning off the car, I hope it's big and hot and eternal and that she's in it.

They were almost to the counter, holding hands. When Randle saw him enter, she looked away; he saw her fingers squeeze Alex's, twice and slow. What was it like for her? Middleman. Alex was staring at the wall menu as if he could read. "I'll get a booth," Mitch said.

A table, instead; there were no empty booths. One by one Alex crumbled the chocolate chip cookies, licked his fingers to dab up the crumbs. Mitch drank coffee.

"That's making me sick," he said to Randle.

Her quick sideways look at Alex. "What?" through half a mouthful, a tiny glob of tartar sauce rich beside her lower lip.

"That smell," nodding at her sandwich. "Fish."

Mouth abruptly stretched, chewed fish and half-smeared sauce, he really was going to be sick. Goddamned *bitch*. Nudging him under the table with one bare foot. Laughing into her Coke.

"Do you always have to make it worse?"

Through another mouthful, "It can't get any worse." To Alex, "Eat your cookies."

Mitch drank more coffee; it tasted bitter, boiled. Randle stared over his head as she ate: watching the patrons? staring at the wall? Alex coughed on cookie crumbs, soft dry cough. Gagged a little. Coughed harder.

"Alex?" Randle put down her sandwich. "You OK? Slap his back," commandingly to Mitch, and he did, harder as Alex kept coughing, almost a barking sound now and heads turned, a little, at the surrounding tables, the briefest bit of notice that grew more avid as Alex's distress increased, louder whoops and Randle suddenly on her feet, trying to raise him up as Mitch saw the first flecks of blood.

"Oh *shit,*" but it was too late, Alex spitting blood now, spraying it, coughing it out in half-digested clots as Randle, frantic, working to haul him upright as Mitch in some stupid reflex swabbed with napkins at the mess. Tables emptied around them. Kids crying, loud and scared, McDonald's employees surrounding them but not too close, Randle shouting, "Help me, you asshole!" and Mitch in dumb paralysis watched as a tiny finger, red but recognizable, flew from Alex's mouth to lie wetly on the seat.

Hammerlock, no time to care if it hurt him, Randle already slamming her back against the door to hold it open and Alex's staining gurgle hot as piss against his shoulder, Randle screaming "Give me the keys! Give me the keys!" Her hand digging hard into his pocket as he swung Alex, whitefaced, into the backseat, lost his balance as the car jerked into gear and fell with the force of motion to hit his temple, dull and cool, against the lever of the seat release.

And lay there, smelling must and the faint flavor of motor oil, Alex above collapsed into silence, lay a long time before he finally thought to ask, "Where're we going?" He had to ask it twice to cut the blare of the radio.

Randle didn't turn around. "Hope there's nothing in that house you wanted."

Night, and the golden arches again. This time they ate in the car, taking turns to go inside to pee, to wash, the restrooms small as closets. Gritty green soap from the dispenser. Alex ate nothing. Alex was still asleep.

Randle's lolling glance, too weary to sit up straight any more. "You drive for awhile," she said. "Keep on I-10 till you get—"

"I know," louder than he meant; he was tired, too. It was a chore just to keep raising his hand to his mouth. Randle was feeling for something, rooting slowly under the seat, in her purse. When he raised his eyebrows at her she said, "You got any cigarettes?"

"Didn't you just buy a pack?"

Silence, then, "I left them at the house. On the back of the toilet," and without fuller warning began to weep, one hand loose against her mouth. Mitch turned his head, stared at the parking lot around them, the fluttering jerk of headlights like big fat clumsy birds. "I'm sick of leaving stuff places," she said. Her hand muffled her voice, made it sound like she spoke from underwater, some calm green place where voices could never go. "Do you know how long I've been wearing this shirt?" and before he could think if it was right to give any answer, "Five days. That's how long. Five fucking days in this same fucking shirt."

From the backseat Alex said, "Breaux Bridge," in a tone trusting and tender as a child's. Without turning, without bothering to look Randle pistoned her arm in a backhand punch so hard Mitch flinched watching it.

Flat-voiced, "You just shut up," still without turning, as if the backseat had become impossible for her. "That's all you have to do. Just shut up."

Mitch started the car. Alex began to moan, a pale whimper that undercut the engine noise. Randle said, "I don't care what happens, don't wake me up." She pulled her T-shirt over her head and threw it out the window.

"Randle, for God's sake! At least wait till we get going."

"Let them look." Her breasts were spotted in places, a rashy speckle strange in the greenish dashlight, like some intricate tattoo the details of which became visible only in hard daylight. She lay with her head on his thigh, the flesh beneath her area of touch asleep before she was. He drove for almost an hour before he lightly pushed her off.

And in the backseat the endless sound of Alex, his rustling paper, the marshy odor of his tears. To Mitch it was as if the envelope of night had closed around them not forever but for so long there was no difference to be charted or discerned. Like the good old days. Like Alex staggering around and around, newspaper carpets and the funnies especially, vomiting blood that eclipsed the paler smell of pigeon shit from the old pigeon coop. Pigeonnier. Black dirt, alluvial crumble and sprayed like tarot dust across the blue-tiled kitchen floor. Wasn't it strange that he could still remember that tile, its gaudy Romanesque patterns? Remember it as he recalled his own nervous shiver, hidden like treasure behind the mahogany boards. And Randle's terrified laughter. Momma. Promises, his hands between her dusty palms; they were so small then, his hands. Alex wiping uselessly at the scabby drip of his actions, even then you had to watch him all the time. Broken glasses, one after another. Willow bonfires. The crying cicadas, no, that was happening now, wasn't it? Through the Buick's open windows. Through the hours and hours of driving until the air went humid with daylight and the reeking shimmer of exhaust, and Randle stirring closed-eyed on the front seat beside him and murmuring, anxious in her sleep, "Alex?"

He lay one hand on her neck, damp skin, clammy. "Shhhh, he's all right. It's still my turn. He's all right."

And kept driving. The rustle of paper in the backseat. Alex's soft sulky hum, like some rare unwanted engine that no lack of fuel could hamper, that no one could finally turn off.

And his hands on the wheel as silent as Randle's calmed breathing, as stealthy as Alex's cities, the litany begun anew: Florien, Samtown, Echo, Lecomte, drifting forward like smoke from a secret fire, always burning, like the fires on the levees, like the fire that took their home. Remember that? Mouth open, catching flies his mother would have said. Blue flame like a gas burner. What color does blood burn?

And his head hanging down as if shamefaced, as if dunned and stropped by the blunt hammer of anger, old anger like the fires that never burned out. And his eyes closing, sleeping, though he woke to think Pull over, had to, sliding heedless as a drunken man over to the shoulder to let himself fall, forehead striking gentle against the steering wheel as if victim of the mildest of accidents. Randle still asleep on the seat beside. Alex, was he still saying his cities? Alex? Paper to play with? "Alex," but he spoke the word without authority, in dream against a landscape not welcome but necessary: in which the rustle of Alex's paper mingled with the slower dribble of his desires, the whole an endless pavane danced through the cities of Louisiana, the smaller, the hotter, the better. And he, and Randle too, were somehow children again, kids at the old house where the old mantle of protection fell new upon them, and they unaware and helpless of the burden, ignorant of the loss they had already and irrevocably sustained, loss of life while living it. You have to swear me, Michie. And Randle, not Randle then, not Francey but Marie-Claire, that was her name, Marie-Claire promising as he did, little sister with her hands outstretched.

The car baked slow and thorough in the shadeless morning, too far from the trees. Alex, grave as a gargoyle chipped cunningly free, rose, in silence the backdoor handle and through the open windows his open palms, let the brownish flakes cascade down upon Mitch and Randle both, swirling like the glitter snow in a paperweight, speckles, freckles, changing to a darker rain, so lightly they never felt it, so quiet they never heard. And gone.

The slap of consciousness, Randle's cry, disgust, her hands grubby with it, scratching at the skin of her forearms so new blood rose beneath the dry. Scabbed with blood, painted with it. Mitch beside her, similarly scabbed, brushing with a detached dismay, not quite fastidious, as if he was used to waking covered with the spoor of his brother's predilections.

"I'm not his mother!" Screaming. She was losing it, maybe already had. Understandable. Less so his own lucidity, back calm against the seat; shock free? Maybe he was crazier than she was. Crazier than Alex, though that would be pushing it. She was still screaming, waves of it that shook her breasts. He was getting an erection. Wasn't that something.

"I'm sick of him being a monster! I can't—"

"We have to look for him."

"You look! You look! I'm tired of looking!" Snot on her lips. He grabbed her by the breasts, distant relish, and shoved her very hard against the door. She stopped screaming and started crying, a dry drone that did not indicate if she had actually given in or merely cracked. Huh-huh-huh. "Put your shirt on," he said, and remembered she didn't have one, she had thrown it away. Stupid bitch. He gave her his shirt, rolled his window all the way down. Should they drive, or go on foot? How far? How long had they slept? He remembered telling her it was his turn to watch Alex. Staring out the window. Willows. Floodplain. Spanish moss. He had always hated Spanish moss. So *hot,* and Randle's sudden screech, he hated that too, hated the way her lips stretched through mucus and old blood and new blood and her pointing finger, pointing at Alex. Walking towards them.

Waving, extravagant, exuberant, carrying something, something it took both hands to hold. Even from this distance Mitch could see that Alex's shirt was soaked. Saturated. Beside him Randle's screech had shrunk to a blubber that he was certain, this time, would not cease. Maybe ever. Nerves, it got on his nerves, mosquito with a dentist's drill digging at your ear. At your brain. At his fingers on the car keys or maybe it was just the itch of blood as he started the car, started out slow, driving straight down the middle of the road to where he, and Randle, and Alex, slick and sticky to the hairline, would intersect. His foot on the gas pedal was gentle, and Alex's gait rocked like a chair on the porch as he waved his arms again, his arms and the thing within.

Randle spoke, dull through a mouthful of snot. "Slow down," and he shook his head without looking at her, he didn't really want to see her at this particular moment.

"I don't think so," he said, as his foot dipped, elegant, like the last step in a dance. Behind Alex, the diagonal shadows of willow trees, old ones; sturdy? Surely. There was hardly any gas left in the car, but he had just enough momentum for all of them.

Angels in Love

L IKE WINGS. Rapturous as the muted screams, lush the beating of air through chipboard walls, luscious like sex and oh, my, far more forbidden: whatever it was, Lurleen *knew* it was wrong.

Knew it from the shrieks, gagged and that was no pillow, no sir no way, she herself was familiar with the gasp of muffled sex and this was definitely not it. And not—really—kinky, or not in any way she knew of, and with a half-shy swagger Lurleen could admit she had acquaintance of a few. Kiss me here. Let's see some teeth. Harder.

The sounds, arpeggio of groans, that basso almost-unheard thump, thump, rhythmic as a headboard or a set of baritone springs but that wasn't it either. Subsonic; felt by the bones. Lying there listening her own bones tingled, skin rippled light with goosebumps, speculation: who made those strange strange sounds? Someone with a taste for the rough stuff, maybe, someone who liked the doughy strop of flesh. Someone strong. An old boyfriend had used to say she fucked like an angel, she never understood the phrase till now. Her hands, deliberate stroll southward, shimmy of familiar fingers on as-familiar flesh; her own groans in counterpoint to the ones through the walls.

Waking heavy in the morning, green toothpaste spit and trying to brush her hair at the same time, late again. "You're late," Roger would say when she walked in, and she would flip fast through her catalog of excuses, which hadn't he heard lately? and try to give him something to get her by, thinking all the while of last night's tingle, puzzling again its ultimate source. It was kind of a sexy game to Lurleen, that puzzling; it gave her something to do at work.

Music store. No kind of music she liked but sometimes it wasn't too bad, and the store itself had a kind of smell that she enjoyed, like a library smell, like something educational was going on. Sheet music, music stands, Roger fussy with customers, turning the stereo on loud and saying stuff like, "But have you heard Spivakov's Bach? Really quite good," like he had probably heard Bach's Bach and could have suggested a few improvements. Right.

Today she felt, was, dopey and sluggish, simple transactions done twice and twice wrong; Roger was pissed, glowered as she slumped through the day. At quitting time he made a point of pointedly disappearing, not saying goodnight; sighing, she had to find him, hide and seek through the racks, he was a stickler for what he called the pleasantries: Goodnight, Lurleen. Goodnight, Roger. Every day.

Finally: hunched behind the order counter, flipping through the day's mail like he hadn't read it nine times already. Lurleen leaned tippy-toe over, flathanded on the cracking gray laminate: "Goodnight, Roger."

Chilly nod, like he'd just caught her trying to palm something: "Goodnight, Lurleen." Waited till she was almost out the door to say, "Lurleen?"

Stopped, impatient keys in hand. "What?"

"We open at ten o'clock. Every day."

Asshole. "See you tomorrow," not banging the door, giving herself points for it. Outside her skin warmed, like butter, spread velvet all over, he always kept the fucking store too cold. Like the music'd melt or something if he turned it up past freezing. Rolling all her windows down, singing to the Top 40 station. Stopped at the party store for cigarettes and to flirt with the clerk, old guy just about as ugly as Roger but round where Roger was slack, furry where Roger was not.

"You headin' out tonight?" sliding the cigarettes across the counter, grinning at her tits. "Have some fun?"

"Oh, I always manage to have fun," over the shoulder smile as she headed for the door, Roger liked to stare at her tits too, she was positive, she just hadn't caught him at it yet. Asshole probably went home and jerked off, dreaming about her bouncing around to Bach. And she laughed, a little: who'd been flying solo last night, huh? But that was different.

In the dark, blind witness to the nightly ravishment, Lurleen, closed eyes, busy hands filling in the blanks, timing herself to the thump and stutter of the rapture beyond the walls. Longer tonight, ecstatic harmony of gulping cries, and after the crescendo wail, soundtrack to her own orgasm, she slept: to dream of flesh like iron, of rising whole, and drenched, and shiny-bright; shock-heavy with a pleasure poisonously rare. Woke just in time to see that she'd slept through the clock. Again.

In the hallway, pausing—already late, so what if she was later—before the door next door. Identical in nondescription to every other down the grimy hall, there was no way to tell by looking just what kind of fun went on there every night. Lurleen, tapping ignition key to lips, thoughtful sideways stare. Imagining, all the reluctant way to work, what sort of exotica, what moist brutalities were practiced there, what kinds of kinks indulged. Wriggling a little, skirt riding up and the cracked vinyl edges of the too-hot seat pressing voluptuously sharp into the damp flesh of her thighs.

It came to her that she had never really seen that next-door neighbor of hers. Maybe they'd bumped into each other, exchanged laundry-room hellos, but for the life of her Lurleen could not recall. She wasn't even sure if it was just one person or a couple. They sure were a couple at night, though, weren't they just.

The day spent avoiding Roger's gaze, colder than the store and just as constant, more than one smart remark about time clocks. Stopping for cigarettes, she picked up a six-pack too, clandestine sips at red lights, rehearsing queenly answers she would never give. It was so hot outside it felt good, brought a warm slow trickle of sweat down the plane of her temple, the hotter spot between her breasts.

She was going out tonight, that was for sure, she owed herself something for the just-past bitch of a day. Walking up the two flights a thought nudged her, firm and brisk to get past the beer. She leaned to sight up the stairwell, heart a trifle nervous, quick and jangly in her chest. Well. No time like the present, was there, to scratch a little itch? I'll just say hi, she thought, walking quicker now. I'll say, Hi, I'm your next-door neighbor, I just stopped by to say hello.

Fourth can in hand, smart tattoo on the door before she could change her mind. Wondering who would open, what they would look like. What they would smell like—Lurleen was a great believer in smells. If they would ask her in, and what she might say, knowing she would say yes and a smile past the thick spot in her throat, and she smiled at that, too, it wasn't that big a deal, was it?

Maybe it was.

Nothing. Silence inside so she knocked again, louder, humming to herself and oh boy here we go: winded swing of the door and "Hi," before it was all the way open. "Hi, I'm Lurleen, your neighbor?"

Tall, her first thought. And skinny. Not model-skinny, just chicken bones, short blonde hair, Giants T-shirt over a flat chest. Anne, the girl said her name was, and past her curved shoulders Lurleen could see a flat as cramped and dingy as her own, a little emptier, maybe, a little less ripe, but nothing special. Purely ordinary. Like Anne herself: no exotic bruising, no secret sheen. Just stood there in the doorway playing with the end of her baggy T-shirt, flipping it as she talked and that thin-lipped smile that said Are you ready to leave yet? Just one big disappointment, but Lurleen didn't show it, kept up her own smile through the strain of the stillborn chatter until she was back inside her own place, sucking up the last of her beer.

"Well," through a closed-mouth ladylike burp. "Well."

How could someone so dull have such a wild sex life? Be better off meeting the boyfriend, he had to be the real show. Fucking angel. Lurleen's giggles lasted through the rest of the beer, her long cool shower and half-hour's worth of mousse and primp. When she left for the bar Anne's flat was silent still, not even the requisite TV drone. From the parking lot the lifeless drift of her curtains, beige to Lurleen's red, was all there was to see.

At the bar she met a couple of guys, nice ones, she couldn't quite remember which was Jeff and which was Tony, but they kept her dancing, and drinking, and that was nice, too. After last call she swiveled off her seat, sweet and smiled and said she was sorry but she had an hour to make the airport to pick up her husband, and even as she said it she had to wonder why; it was one of them she'd planned on picking up, and never mind that she couldn't remember who was who, names didn't exactly matter at that time of night, words didn't matter past Who's got the rubber. But still she left alone.

KATHE KOJA

Coming home, off-center slew into her parking space, radio up way too loud, singing and her voice a bray in the cut-engine quiet; she almost slipped going up the stairs. Shushing herself as she poured a glass of milk, her invariable after binge cure-all. Lifting the glass she caught from the damp skin of her forearm an aftershave scent, mixed with the male smell of Tony. Jeff? It didn't matter, such a pretty boy.

But not as pretty as the boy next door.

And, her thought seeming eerily a signal, she heard the preliminary noises, shifting warm through the wall as if they stroked her: Anne's breathy wordless voice, that rush of sound, half-sinister whirlwind pavane. Pressed against the wall itself, her bare-skinned sweat a warm adhesive, Lurleen stood, mouth open and eyes shut, working her thin imagination as Anne, presumably, worked her thin body, both— all three—ending in vortex, whirlpool, mouthing that dwindling symphony of screams, Lurleen herself louder than she'd ever been, with any man. Loud enough that they could, maybe, hear her through the walls.

Slumped, damp, she could not quite admit it, say to herself You want them to hear you. You want him to hear you, whoever he is. You want what Anne's getting, better than any bar pickup, better than anything you ever had. Glamorous and dirty. And scary. And hot.

By the next night she was ready, had turned her bed to face the wall lengthwise: willing herself, forcing herself like an unseen deliberate splinter in their shared and coupling flesh—she would be part of this. She had never had anything like what went on there, never anything good. She would have this if she had to knock down the wall to get it. Fingers splayed against her flesh, heels digging hard into the sheets and letting go, crying out, hear me. Hear me.

Exhausted at work, but on time, she couldn't take any of Roger's bitching now, not when she had to think. Make a plan. Anne, she was a sorry-looking bitch, no competition once the boyfriend got a good look at Lurleen. The trick was to get him to look. To see. See what he'd been hearing, night after night. Of course it wouldn't be all that easy, if Anne had any brains she would want to keep her boyfriend and Lurleen far far apart. Lurleen decided she would have to take it slow and smart, be smart, not exactly her strong point but she could be slick, she knew what she wanted.

She began to stalk Anne, never thinking of it in so many words but as sure and surely cautious as any predator. Waiting, lingering in the hallway after work, for Anne to come home from whatever unfathomable job she did all day. Never stopping to talk, just a smile, pleasant make-believe. She made it her business to do her laundry when Anne did hers; at the first whoosh and stagger of the old machine Lurleen was there, quarters in hand; her clothes had never been so clean; she had to see. Any jockey shorts, bikini underwear, jockstraps, what? She meant to take one if she could, steal it before, before it was clean. Smell it. You can tell a lot about a man, Lurleen believed, from the smell of his skin, not his aftershave or whatever but the pure smell of his body. Until his body was beneath hers it was the best she could do. She pawed through the laundry basket, poked around in the washer: nothing. Just Anne's Priss-Miss blouses, baggy slacks, cheap bras, and just about everything beige. Balked angry toss of the clothing, stepped on it to push it back into the basket. Maybe he liked Anne because she was so beige, so . . . nothing? Could a man want a woman to be nothing? Just a space to fill? Lurleen had known plenty of guys who liked their women dumb, it made them feel better, but anyway Anne didn't seem dumb. Just empty.

And still, night after night the same, bed against the wall, Lurleen could be determined, Lurleen could work for what she wanted. Drained every morning, the sting of tender skin in the shower, even Roger noticed her red eyes.

"Not moonlighting, are you," but she saw he knew it was no question, half-gaze through those tired eyes and she even, for a moment, considered telling him, considered saying I want the boy next door, Roger, I want him real bad. I want him so much I even jerk off so he can hear me, so he can know how he turns me on. I want him so much I don't know what to do.

She wasn't getting anywhere. Drumming slow one finger against the order counter, staring right past some guy bumbling on about some opera or something, she wasn't getting anywhere and it was wearing her out. No time for anything else, bars, guys, whatever, there wasn't any other guy she wanted. Anne's smiles growing smaller, tighter, her gaze more pinched, was she catching on? Tired from sitting in the hallway, once or twice another neighbor had caught her at it, loitering tense and unseeing until the tap-tap-tap on her shoulder, Hey are you OK? "Fine," harsh involuntary blush, "just looking for an earring." Right. Tired from staking out the parking lot, hot breeze through the window; she didn't even know what kind of car he drove. Tired to death and still no glimpse of him, proud author of the sounds, it was killing her to listen but she couldn't stop. She didn't want to stop.

And then that night, mid-jerk, mid-groan, they stopped. The sounds. Ceased completely but not to complete silence, a waiting sound, a whisper. Whispering through the walls, such a willing sound.

She yanked on a T-shirt, ends tickling her bare ass as she ran, hit on the door with small quick fists, "Anne? Are you OK?" never thinking how stupid she might look if the door opened, never considered what excuse she might give. I didn't hear anything so I thought you might be in trouble. Right. So what. Bang bang on the door.

"Anne?"

The whisper, against the door itself. Hearing it Lurleen shivered, convulsive twitch like a tic of the flesh, all down her body and she pressed against the door, listening with all her might. "Anne," but quietly, feeling the heat from her body, the windy rush of her heart. Waiting. "Anne," more quietly still, less than a murmuring breath, "let me in."

Abruptly, spooking her back a step: the sounds, hot, intensity trebled but wrong somehow, guttural, staggering where they should flow, a smell almost like garbage but she didn't care, once the first scare had passed she pressed harder into the door, as if by pure want she could break it down, she would get in, she would. T-shirt stuck, sweating like she'd run a mile. I'm sick of just listening. The hall was so hot. Sweat on her forehead, running into her eyes like leaking tears. The doorknob in her slick fingers.

It turned. Simple as that.

In the end so quick and easy and it seemed almost that she could not breathe, could not get enough air to move but she moved all right, oh yes, stepped right inside into the semidarkness, a fake hurricane lamp broken beside the bed but there was light enough, enough to see by.

Like angels in love, mating in the cold graceful rapture of thin air. Hovering above the bed, at least a yard or maybe more, no wonder she never heard springs, instead the groaned complaint of the walls itself as his thrusting brushed them, on his back the enormous strange construction that kept them airborne, as careless as if it had grown there amongst the pebbled bumps and tiny iridescent fins.

His body beautiful, and huge, not like a man's but so real it seemed to suck up all the space in the room, big elementary muscles and he was using them all. Anne, bent like a coat hanger, it hurt to see the angle of her back, her eyes wide and empty and some stuff coming out of her mouth like spoiled black jelly but it was too late, Lurleen had sent the door swinging backwards to close with a final catch, and in its sound his gaze swiveling to touch hers: the cold regard of a nova, the summoning glance of a star.

Her mouth as open as Anne's as she approached the vast brutality of his embrace, room enough for two there, oh my yes. Fierce relentless encroachment promising no pleasure but the pleasure of pain. Not an angel, never had been. Or maybe once, long, a long long time ago.

Waking the Prince

IN HIS BEAUTY SO PALE, the pallor of false dawn beneath glass smooth and cold as his skin, ceremonial glass on which one sees the imprint of many kisses, fingertips, palm prints pressed to warm what cannot be warmed, evidence of balked desire for what lies so deceptively near. White and rapt and naked past that barrier unseen, long limbs, knees and elbows slightly bent, hair the color of cinnamon on his chest and legs, nestled wiry about his manhood which sleeps as well. There is, it seems, in the air above the case the faintest odor: as of sachet, or dried cosmetics, or sweets crushed dry and secret in a drawer; not everyone can smell it, but for those who can its scent is maddening, a delicious corruption, the body unrisen decomposed to candied light.

The case, or casket, lies beneath a heavy canopy, gilt and royal purple, flags and tassels and shiny bunting; he is a king's son after all, will be, yes, king himself should his father die, his father who in a mounting rictus of dry despair can bear to spend no time within the same walls that house his son, has moved both hearth and seat of government to a manor house some leagues away, where he eats, sleeps, keeps a mistress—but like a curse fulfilled, some wicked habit irresistible still returns to stand in that hall, before that case and on his face gall-bitter the chase and crawl of his thoughts: How many hours, how much of life lost already, young life lost and gone and bent crooning like a nursemaid, crooning curses like a soul damned to hell and "This is hell," His Grace's mutter, "*this* is hell," to his son's slack sleeping face, shaped both of beauty and death; perhaps it is that irony as much as her husband's slow decampment which has driven the queen his mother mad.

See her: as around the barbican she creeps, up and down the twilight halls in red gown and clattering boots, hair loose down her back as if she were a girl, a maiden unwed and *Who has stolen it?* she says, to the walls, to herself, her voice the voice of fever and disease, of the sore that grows like hunger in the spread feast of the flesh, insisting in her mania that her son is jailed, locked inside the case: glass case which bears no seals, no seams, no indication of manufacture as if it had always been there, had formed cold and strong as a carapace about the sleeping body of the beautiful prince. *Who has stolen the key?* for she insists there is a key, one true key the presence of which will bring to light the lock unseen, will turn that lock, will free her boy from his silence and his pallor, her naked son in the glass cask of that womb. She hears no other voices, will listen to no one—the vizier or maidservants, ladies-in-waiting or her husband the King who, when confronted by fresh evidence of her madness limits his answer to a shrug: "What will you?" to that vizier, those maidservants weeping into their cupped palms as if kept tears will solve the matter. "Scamper like a rat, crawl like a snake, what matter? She is broken, inside; let her be."

The queen in torment; the king in hiding; the kingdom captive beneath the lids of the sleeping prince. Outside the palace the gardeners tend the gravel paths, the massed banks of flowers: lily, aster, kiss-me-quick; inside the wine steward checks the vintage for the evening meal.

"So what's he like?" Tanisha's question to Cissy sitting on the floor: beer sucked through a straw, gold bubbles, gold earrings to swing and dangle, make motion in the motionless air. "This guy, he's an actor, you said?"

"He's in commercials." More beer sucked through that smile; she felt as if she had been smiling ever since they met. "He did that one for Edie's IceDream, you know the one with the guys on the lake? And they all fall in the water? well he's the third guy, the one in the bandanna. The perfect one."

Inner squint of memory: "They're all perfect."

"Well, he's *perfect*-perfect." Dark hair, dark eyes and that heavy underlip like a child's, pouting child too sweet to be called spoiled. Picked out like pure gold in a box of fakes, kick of instinct there in the thrash bar angled up against the rail; *finders keepers,* Cissy's smile and moving closer, watching him watch her walk. Glass in hand, gin and grapefruit juice cloudy and sour and he had let her taste it, one swirling sip and "You like it?" with half a smile. "Like how it tastes?"

"Sure," and his arm around her, casual across her shoulder, above her beating heart. "It's, it's different," and he had laughed, bright laugh as if what she had said was a joke and "He's different," she said now to Tanisha, "he's not like anybody else."

"One of a kind, huh?" Nodding to the empty can: "You want another one of these?"

"No. —Yeah, I'll split one with you but then I gotta go, I gotta get ready." For tonight, another night and again the reminiscent smile: sour grapefruit aftertaste, head to one side and at first she had tried to be cool, not wanting to smile too much, get too close too soon but oh he was so beautiful, perfect like a magazine model, like on TV and naked even better, her own mouth sucking sweet on that underlip, biting like ripe fruit and afterwards lying on his belly in her bed, pink sheets and his skin the color of caramel, of honey in the comb. Like a wish you make, genie in the lamp, what's your pleasure? and "—body home? Hello?" and Tanisha was handing her the beer can, pushing it cold and smooth into her hand. "So you going out with him again tonight?"

"Dancing," she said. "We're going dancing." Her suggestion: said into silence, you like to dance? and he had shrugged and smiled, lying present-wrapped, pink-swaddled in the sheets, lids low and lower, closing as if draped at last by dream: had he answered, yes or no? Yes. No.

Consultations have been made, of course; priests and witches and necromancers, scores of them, lines of them to advise Their Majesties: spells tried, prayers and incantations, the burned flesh of beasts on altars but all without effect and these efforts then devolving to applications of more temporal force: iron and fire, saws and cunning tools made to cut rock, six strong men with leaden bars to batter like thunder against the glass, the queen in the room's far corner weeping alternately from hope and terror, *oh have a care, have a care!*—but the sweat flew to no effect, the tools lay blunted, the bars themselves left bent and shattered in a corner of the room.

In the arched doorway the queen cries out once, as a woman in labor cries out in the tunnel of birth: and then is gone, off on her endless rounds, stubborn as the prince himself: more opinions sought and solicited, ears cracked for any whisper no matter how unpleasant or bizarre and finally anyone with a plan is allowed to enter and speak, in these last mad days before the king's decampment, before the queen is swallowed whole by her grief: the mountebanks and beggars, the deranged, the ones said to be gifted by second sight, the ones with extra fingers or missing legs and through the halls they move, pilfering, loitering, stealing food from the kitchens, their sticks and bloody bones playing that tune peculiar to the halt, the ones not whole and across the glass sarcophagus they clamber, slack and shivering limbs in an insect's communion, the feeder and the fed: but even those grotesqueries mean nothing, nothing changes and in the halls still the weeping queen, the king enraged, the prince sealed and sleeping in his transparent tomb as if he will sleep forever, as if not even death can wake him now.

Well then, not *perfect* after all: her sweet actor turned out to be a lousy dancer, pure wood which was somehow endearing, his one fault but how could she care when everything else was so right? And anyway who needed to go dancing, the important thing was to spend time together, be with him every minute she could and she did what she could, late to work and leaving early, spare clothes in her tote bag so she didn't have to go home first, could head straight to his place, be there waiting when he got back: from the studio, from a shoot, this week it was work boots for some outdoor-fashion magazine and to see him coming towards her, coming up the street made Cissy feel as if she had won the lotto, luck's blessing like a magic wand and *his* magic wand, oh yeah, blessings of another kind and they spent hours in bed, her hands learning the landscape of that body, what he liked, what he needed—the little tweaks and touches, the way he liked her to whisper what he wanted her to say—and afterwards he always slept, little catnaps and she would lie beside him and look, just look, just watch him doze and think to herself *this is it:* past definition to surety, her head beside his on the pillow, pillowed on a sweetness she had not imagined: nothing like this had ever happened to her before, and nothing she did or could do would be too much: to keep it all happening, to keep him here.

And Tanisha on the phone, other friends, girlfriends asking with a mixture of envy and delight So how's it goin'? Still good? and "Great," she told them, told Tanisha over coffee, too hot and gulped too fast but she was in a hurry, she was meeting him for dinner: "At Pumpernickel's," shucking shoes under the table, tired feet slipping into cool pumps carried careful in her bag all day. "We're celebrating, it's six months today." Six months of good times, well almost all but it all took a lot of work, a lot of planning and traveling around but it was nothing to complain about, not really because she was so lucky to have him and now Tanisha, stirring coffee and "You talked any more about moving in?" Gritty sugar spill, wind chime sound of the spoon. "Remember you said you were going to?"

"Yeah, I—yeah, we did." Changing earrings, gold studs for flashy gold hoops and they *had* talked about it, she had talked plenty but to everything she said that shrug, sweet smile and it ended like it always did, everything in the end down to pink sheets and catnap yawns. So "We decided to wait awhile," another gulp of coffee, burning her mouth, her throat going down. "I mean he really likes his place, you know, and I like mine, so we'll just wait."

Tanisha's gaze, calm and dry and something else and "What?" Cissy said, a little too sharp. "What's that look for?"

"Nothing," said Tanisha. "Just, you look kind of, you know, tired. You getting enough sleep?"

"Long day," with her own gaze level and cool, "just a long day," which by the time she hit the restaurant was longer; his job to make the reservations but he had forgotten: again:

and she had to wait for a table, sit there drinking water and wondering, wondering but finally here he came: and that lift inside, dependable as physics to see him cross the room, hands in his pockets and leaning like ballet to kiss her, careless kiss on half her mouth and "You're late," she said, surprising them both, it was not what she meant to say at all and he lifted his eyebrows, leaned back and smiled.

"Traffic," he said. "I had to come across town," and then busy with the menu, busy with his drink when it came, *happy anniversary* and she decided to bring it up again, moving in: six months was a long time after all. "You know I've been thinking," she said. "About what we said, you know, about us moving in together," and step by step her careful logic, money saved, less travel time meant more time together, so on and so forth and it really sounded good, no it sounded *right*, she *was* right and turning now in the slippery leather booth, wedging sideways to look into his eyes—to see him looking past her, peaceable over her shoulder; one hand loose around the wine glass, the other warm around hers and he could have been sleeping, he could have been on the moon or a million miles away and some sound made, some noise because "What?" his head swiveling toward her, smile like a distracted child's. "What is it, babe?" and then the waitress with their dinner, flat red plates, burned smell and Nothing, she said; had she said it aloud? "Nothing," more firmly but now he was joking with the waitress, he was not listening, he had not been listening at all.

It has been rumored that His Grace is considering some action, one last plan which would bring to the situation if not peace then resolution of a sort, yet when it comes the announcement is its own surprise: All of them, court and kind, lords and maidservants are to be removed to the former hunting lodge, now officially the royal residence; this castle is to be if not strictly abandoned then certainly shuttered, manned by a staff of no more than five to keep the building free of tramps or vandals; the rest will accompany the king and court to what His Grace calls, with a cynic's hope, the kingdom's new home.

No one says it aloud, no one asks in words but *What of the prince?* to one another, said with their gazes, their lowered lids and "What of Her Grace?" asks the vizier, voice free of opinion, alone with the king in what had once been the privy chamber. "Does she approve of this action?"

"It is not her function," says the king, voice heavy and cold, "to approve. Or disapprove."

"Then she will be—leaving, as well?"

"And why should she not, my Lord Vizier?" the king close and closer, breath warm as an animal's, thick with wine against the vizier's cheek. "What holds her here?" and the vizier knows that now the prince is to be understood as dead by all but those five unfortunates, that wretched staff left behind like curs in a kennel to tend what asks no tending, to watch what none would steal. "Nothing," says the vizier, gaze calm upon the king. "Forgive my lack of understanding."

And now past the locked doors they hear it, the sound of passage: ragged gown and boots gone heelless, the queen stumbling down the hall and the vizier says nothing, sits inspecting his fingers, the tips of his boots; politely, as one avoids noticing another's poverty, another's idiot child. It is murmured that in her spiraling torment Her Grace has passed through darker gates, places no Christian should go; some claim they have seen men moving about the palace at night, when all but Her Grace are in slumber, men in dark cloaks who wear—are they?—masks like the heads of goats, men who make no sound as they pass but hear her now, rush and stagger and the king rising, pushing at the table and in this light it is impossible even for the vizier not to mark how he has aged, His Grace, aged badly past pity or help and "I will speak to the chamberlain," says the vizier, moving now towards the door in the wake of the king who moves as if to his own death, a slow and tired motion grotesque in a man of his years. "There is much to be done."

At the doorway the king turns, one hand poised on the jamb: "See the place is emptied in a fortnight," and now the open door, the hall: to the left the dying sounds of the queen's passage, to the right the branching turn which leads to the room with the glass case, the shadows and the silence and with great delicacy, the vizier looking neither right nor left. "Her Grace has been—informed?"

No sound at all, there in the early darkness.

"I will tell her now," says the king.

"Remember I told you," Cissy still smiling; like lifting weights, but still a smile. "March twenty-fourth. It's Jenny's wedding, and it's going to be black tie, so you need to rent your tux pretty soon. OK?"

"Mmm," rolling over, eyes closed and she said it again, "March twenty-fourth, don't forget" and "Who's Jenny?" he asked. Sirens outside, clipping past and "You know who she is," trying not to sound angry, trying to sound like nothing at all. "My sister's girl. My niece." Stepniece, stepdaughter, so what; family was family and she wanted to show him off, black tie and "Don't forget," she said, "OK? This is important, write it down or something," which was ridiculous, he never wrote anything down: I keep it all up here, he would say, sweet curve of that smiling mouth— and then the wasted theater tickets, the broken dates and missed dinners, weren't you listening? and his kiss, his shrug, he was always sorry, he always said he was sorry.

"Please," she said: black-and-white quilt like a checkerboard drawn up over his chin; like a kid, a little kid and "So he's going?" Tanisha at lunch, kiosk sandwiches in the snowflake drift, Cissy's ungloved fingers red and stiff and "Sure," she said, "sure he's going," not looking at Tanisha because Tanisha had heard this particular refrain before but this time, "This time," she said, "is different. Because he knows, all right? He knows how important it is."

"Well sure," Tanisha said. Coffee gone cold in the styrofoam cups; her careful smile. "It's an important day."

Don't remind him: like a mantra, *don't remind him anymore* and she said nothing, only circled the date, big red circle and a big red J on the supermodel calendar he kept in the kitchen and "So are we finally going to meet this guy?" her sister in the store, they had picked out their dresses: mother-of-the-bride in tasteful ecru, Cissy in strapless black and "Mom's dying to see him," her sister said. "Listen, is he really that gorgeous? Mom said you said he was perfect."

Half-closed eyes, black and white; yes and no. "Yes," she said, "he really is," and that night she showed him the dress, tried it on: strapless black, tight across her breasts and "Oh wow," that lazy smile as she turned on her heel, self-conscious pivot like a model, supermodel and "Gorgeous, gorgeous," he said, rising up on one elbow. "So what's the occasion?"

See, then, the caravan: Her Grace in last hoarse protest, bundled dry into the carriage with her maids and ladies, her chaplain and his staff; the last to leave is, of course, the king. Already mounted, looking down at the five who have chosen to stay and "You have all my gratitude," says His

Grace. The horse's steaming breath, the heavy air to threaten snow and then he is gone, joined at a distance by his equerries, their sound the only sound in the landscape made of grey: the dying year hung with grey branches, the dying castle in which all the wings but one have been permanently closed, to save fuel, to allow the dead to bury their dead.

No one visits the room with the glass case.

Before the spring, all of the five have gone.

"You look terrific," her sister said; ladies' room tissues, offering her lipstick again; someone tried to open the door but her palm kept it shut. "But you have to stop crying, OK? 'Cause I have to get out there, I'm paying for all this."

Her smile dry and unhappy, mother of the bride and "You go on," Cissy said, "go on, I'll be out in a minute. I just want to fix myself a little, wash my face—"

"Are you sure?" one hand still on the door but Cissy waved her away, go, go and alone now, water in the basin, borrowed lipstick and "You promised me," not screaming, she had kept her voice reasonable, shaking voice and trembling hands, strapless black and "You promised me!" to his sad shrug: he had not meant to make her angry, had just forgotten, it was hard to remember everything and "Listen," rising to reach for her, take her arm, "listen I can get washed up, you know, in a minute, I can put on a suit or something—"

"No you can't," she had said, with the first of the tears, "it's *black tie,* black tie you son of a bitch," and moving then, out the door and down the stairs and he might have been looking, there at the window, might have watched her drive away but she did not look, did not turn her head to see if he was there. Frost on the windshield, the heater on high; the new dress tight across her breasts, her shoulders smooth and cold as glass, as if no one had ever touched them, as if she had never been touched before. Halfway there she realized that she had left her purse on the counter, but kept on going; she was not going back, not there, not tonight.

Glossed cold with dust the castle floors, the shattered glaze of the windows; inside is only silence, the empty nestle of owls, stray leaves and feathers, the detritus of solitude and light.

Now and then, if anyone were there to see it, the prince in his case is known to smile. Whether or not he dreams, no one can say.

Ballad of the Spanish Civil Guard

THE POET HAS BEAUTIFUL FINGERS, long fingers, fingers like a girl. Paintbrush hands, his father called them, his father being a man of some humor; his mother said no, they were the hands of a musician. Had not the boy loved music early? Before he could talk he was humming the folk songs, songs of nature, the fields, the terrible strange light of the virgin moon; he knew all the words, he could sing them like an expert. He will be a musician one day, said his mother, stroking his hair with her fingers, pulling fondly the strands like raveled string, dark and lank; and he looking up at her through that string, cat's cradle, bridge: hair like cords to bind the soul, that was what the gypsies said. Hair, blood, semen, all of it useful, all of it rich with secrets and with needs.

The moon is not in evidence; there is nothing here but walls, four stone squares in dark abutment, one to the other to the next; his arms ache, his back, the backs of his weary legs. Across the room, there, is a man with a gun; he is smoking a cigarette and eating an orange, spitting the seeds on the floor.

"You want a cigarette?" the guard says.

The poet shakes his head, mouth open a little, and tries to talk; there is blood on his lower lip, itself split almost down the middle; blood on his pale shirt and loose tie, the kind artists wear. The guards had noted that, one to the other, with derision. An artist; a queer, some of them said, *maricas, apios* they called them in Seville; it was understood that many artists were queer.

Orange seeds on the floor; the sound of men laughing, dark and quiet in the corridor. The poet clears his throat as best he can, prefatory to speech; he has had nothing to drink for almost eight hours, since they came to the home of his friends, his protectors. The black squad: silent eyes and hands beneath his damp elbows, to take him away. "Water?" he says to the guard.

The guard has not understood; the poet must speak again, ask, request: "Water?" Words are his metier, his life's blood; he uses them now with caution, with pity, with terror; it is after all his words which have brought him here, to this room with four walls and no moon, cigarette smoke dense and acrid as arsenic, the guard with his orange and his gun. "May I have water, here?"

The guard surveys him, eyes half-closed and in one motion slips the peel denuded between his lips: his whole mouth now one grotesque and pebbled grin, a pumpkin's toothless smile: spits it into his hand and laughs, a little joke on and for himself. "Water?" he says. "Let us see."

The poet's hands twist warm and nervously; there are rings of dried sweat beneath his shirt. They have handled him roughly, true, true also that they have split his lip; but no one has said anything about murder, no one has mentioned the road, the olive groves; the work to be done there. He has heard about the olive groves, about the men come to dig the graves, spade in one hand, bottle in the other and finding, what? The dead uncle, the dead brother, the dead son. These are times not so much perilous as beyond peril; walking through fire, one forgets to fear the singeing of the sleeve. One will be consumed, devoured dry as that orange, there, its poor peel bent awkward and backward and wrong; or one will live. It is really very simple after all.

The guard returns; no, water is not permitted. No. "Cigarette?" in the proffering hand, reiteration of the one solace available. Take it, *el poeta*, it is truly all you are going to get.

It is very hard to smoke with a mouth so sore but he manages; he fears—without shame; this room is too small and too dark for shame, it would be a luxury, a decadence almost into which he must not fall; what room for decadence when panic is at the door?—and fears to say no to the guard's offer; it may do nothing for him in any case but oh, *el poeta*, it is truly all you are going to get. It is a cheap brand of cigarette; on its paper, now, see the bright new stain.

Somewhere down the corridor, a man screams. The poet thinks he can smell olives, their oil crushed colorless, like blood upon his hands.

No more talk from the guard: he sits, legs crossed, so still he might passably be in sleep if it were not for those eyes, never closed, barely shifted. He is not a man, the poet thinks, for much rumination, the habit of thought is simply not there. Open up his head (still whimsy; still desperate; some habits simply will not die) and what would you find? Bullets, their empty lolling roll? A piece of meat, a warm pudenda, what? Remnants of a speech, fragments on one side gold and red, the colors of tympani, martial colors—but on the other side, ah, the cheapest newsprint, foolscap apropos for the task. If he remembered that much, beyond the imprecations, the shouting and the noise; if he even listened to words of the speeches his leaders made.

He had listened, the poet, nervous hands jammed together like little animals crawling one over another, seeking frantic the burrow that is no longer there, destroyed by a foot, a hand, a motion: forward motion, marching to the future. Death is the future, is it not? Everyone's future, reached at different times, by different ends; as inevitable as birth itself, as suffering, as love. Was it not the gypsies who talked of Death as the lover? Death, the beautiful boy unsmiling, in one hand the mace and scepter, in the other his own wet flesh, tumescent, hard with blood; was it then so hard to understand?

No, finally; but acceptance was another matter, he can accept nothing now, the poet, but the hard floor, the scattered scraps of rind like callused flesh torn by Furies not in rage but indifference: one must eat, after all. After all. He smokes the cigarette down to a burn on his trembling finger; the guard's gaze never leaves him once.

He is a Red, they said, a Russian spy; he has done more damage with his pen than others with their guns. *El poeta*, they said, you are a dangerous man; there in the light, they bring their own light with them, they do not fear for him to see their faces; how confident, after all, they all are. Especially the man in the middle, the one with the long slim eyes, long sleepy lids like a cat's, a lizard's in the sun. Very dangerous, he says.

It is not pride that makes him shrug; there is no room for pride here, either, barely room enough for truth but it is truth that moves his trembling shoulders; he is trembling all over, now. "Not dangerous," he says, trying for clarity, trying to move his swollen lips so he will be understood. "The truth is dangerous."

"The truth," says the man in the middle, "is often what you make it. Is that not so?"—not, note, to the men beside him, to the guard now in the doorway who seems almost to have fallen asleep where he stands: it is very late after all. No, this man, this leader speaks to the poet himself, addresses him as cleanly and directly as a pistol shot. "The truth is what is believed to be true. You should know that, Federico."

The use of his name unnerves him; but already he trembles, he is a glass brimful of fear: what more can be done to frighten him, but death? Torture? He thinks of the gypsies again, the music of *cante jondo,* the deep song that cries in black sounds of pain, loss, the sorrow everlasting of love; and yet hearing it, immersed by it, who can sorrow? be sad? It is the music of the blood in the body; or thus it was explained to him. What wild cantos, now, sing his blood, driven by fear, the animal terror of the body confronted by the idea of the end, no more? The gypsies know what death is.

"Is it not so, Federico?" says the narrow-eyed man, and the poet realizes the man has been speaking, all this time, speaking to him and expecting now perhaps an answer. His throat is so dry it clicks when he swallows, a painful click that makes the men smile, grin at him for what they perceive as another manifestation of his fear; but he is not ashamed: why should he not be afraid? Only a fool does not fear. He tries to clear his throat for speech and finds instead it is simply too dry.

Mouth open like a fish, he gestures—earnestly, earnestly; communication is important, even now; especially now. The guard at the door is dispatched for water, returns with a cup full of something wet and warm: for a moment the poet fears his thirst will overcome his judgment, that he will swallow urine, or blood, or whatever foulness is contained in evil joke inside the cup: but it is water, after all, if somewhat warm and none too clear. He drinks it all, forcing himself to go slowly, while the narrow-eyed man watches, arms crossed like a schoolmaster awaiting a pupil's response.

"Now," he says, when the poet has drunk the cup down.

"You will give us your decision, Federico."

The poet is silent; the most important question, or at least the most crucial, of his life; and he does not know what to say. There are no windows here in the room; if only he could see the moon, he might know better, might have some idea what he must do. Under his armpits he smells his own sour sweat; perhaps they will kill him now.

But the narrow-eyed man is not displeased by his silence, or does not seem to be so. Arms crossed, he uncrosses them, scratches himself through the warm brown fabric of his trousers. "We must have an answer," he says. "Danger, like truth, is what you make of it. As is opportunity. You must realize, Federico, it is opportunity we offer to you now." And he smiles, this man, a smile of impatience and vast simplicity, it is all very simple in the end, so simple the poet need not even hear the words again to know them, from the smile itself he knows them, from the word, *dangerous,* spoken so formally before.

"It is not a consideration offered to many," the narrow-eyed man says; his smile has gone. "It is a chance to participate in history, have you thought of that? Your beloved gypsies, Federico, what will become of them in history's waters? Will they swim? Will they drown? Your answer cannot save them—I am sure you know this already, I give nothing away—but it may save you, to immortalize them, perhaps? in poetry? All wars end, Federico, all wars and insurrections. And conversations; this one is ending now. What will you?" and all the men in the room save the poet seem to stand a little taller, holding themselves as if in the wind of history itself.

"What you offer is monstrous," says the poet. "Even you must know that."

"Mother of God," the narrow-eyed man says; finally he

is angry, or at least profoundly annoyed. "Monstrous, not-monstrous, why do you play this game with me now? Either you will do as is suggested or we will kill you, so. You are done writing poems in any case."

Mother of God, Mother of Sorrows, only two days ago—three?—he had stood praying, hands clasped before an image of the Sacred Heart. On the piano, the image benevolent, crying inside and praying, praying without words: asking for: what? What do you want, *el poeta?* You are done writing poems in any case.

The narrow-eyed man does not even shake his head; gestureless, he gestures to the door. "Coffee," he says. "Give him plenty of coffee." The code for an execution, why such coyness now, such brutal tact? do they think he does not know these things? can they imagine for one moment he does not *know?* For one wild instant he dreams a window, a moon, hands bright with weapons in its light: *we have come to save you, Federico, we have come to get you out.*

There is no window; there is no moon. If he could have been saved it would have been accomplished before now; nothing will happen now but the inevitable, as relentless as the last act of a play. He is handcuffed to another man, a teacher with a wooden leg, and together in lockstep both are forced into the waiting car, in the sorrow of the cricket-less night.

He will die, he thinks, like a matador, like Ignacio Sanchez Mejias: *I remember a sad breeze through the olive trees.* Like a matador, like Christ, dying with his hands open in the shadeless midnight of the olive grove. He is not trembling any longer, nor shivering, he barely feels the manacles about his wrists. The teacher is shot dead; his wooden leg is particularly pitiful.

You next, *el poeta.*

What will the gypsies make of his blood, his sweet white bones? He has heard the body voids itself, in death, leaks urine and nightsoil, semen and sweat. All of it has power, all; even his hair against the ground like roots asearch for purchase, dark and hungry motion on the pebbles and the stones; does not the *cante jondo* tell us so? Perhaps they will fashion another poet from his leavings, a stronger man than he. Or perhaps it will be a different species entirely; a warrior, say. He would not be displeased; surely they will know this, divine it in silence and that deepest understanding, swirling twinned to marrow in the bones.

The eager splash of the *Fuente Grande,* that famous spring there at the killing ground; perhaps the gypsies are watching, now, and waiting, patient only for the bullet to begin their work; O remember me! he cries in his heart, as behind him a man curses, the leaves of the olive trees move. Already his fingers lie open like a lotus, long fingers like a flower to mark the spot where they must begin.

Lady Lazarus

THE MAISONETTE WAS COLD, had been cold, it was cold all over London in this winter where every pain was shaped and clear and made of purest ice. Hands on the table, hands on her head, flat hands with palms as still and cold as sarcophagus marble, my Christ was she going to cry again? No. No. She would not cry for him or anyone, bastard, *bastard* and *her*, that woman, she hoped they both died, spending her money in Spain, she hoped they were both dead. The children were asleep; she had just checked them, dim peaceful faces and they did not know about their father, did not know they were better off without him, better off if he were dead.

Ach, du.

Like voices in her head, auditory hallucinations. She did not have them; shock treatments, yes, but she did not have voices in her head or if she did it was poetry's own voice, not the muse but the bloody angel that flies behind it, no hands at all but talons springing bright as broken bones from the seamless flesh of its arms. She had written three poems this week, might write three more; or thirty; they would make her name, she had written that to her mother. Long letters to her mother like blood trailing on the floor, blood on the ice freezing like jelly and she with a stick to pick it up, messing it back and forth in divination and someone—her husband? her father?—pushing the stick from her hands, her cold hands empty again and the stick snapped in half like a broken bone, its lines like runes, instructions in dark angles so subtle and opaque that no one could fail to understand. Voodoo dolls, magic mirrors broken in slivers and slats like the gates of hell, the gates of heaven, all of it power and glory but who had the power, really, and the glory that comes with it like stink comes with shit, who? Not her, there at the table, not her with her head in her hands.

It was two thirty in the morning, temperatures falling cold as old stones, old black stones and she had been trying to write, write a new poem about old black stones. The rooms were clean and quiet; toys and clothes in order, kitchen clean, three cups and one tray of uncooked muffins lying like sacrifice on the minuscule counter. She thought she heard her neighbor stir, downstairs; she thought she heard the baby breathe, his whole pink body one susurrating whisper; thought she heard her daughter sigh in the midst of a dream. Little girls are born with dreams, curled needs inside like little eggs waiting to drop, fall fat like fruit, like the seeds of babies; but they don't need them. What they need are weapons, armies; they need to be armies, they need to be able to fight. Little boys are taught how to do that; it is a knowledge assumed as necessary as knowing how to point your penis when you piss. Learn how to fight, hit, throw stones, black stones like pennies on her eyes, she would lie in a grave like a trundle bed and who would care then? Not him.

Her hand on the paper like automatic writing, like using the planchette, its little needle the pointy nose of some feared pet, grave weasel, ferreting out the damned: you, and you. And you, especially; you didn't think we would forget *you*. She had been writing, trying to write since midnight, since two; she had talked to her neighbor, his face swarming out of the light belowstairs like some bewildered god, a modern god left without magic in the normal miracle of electricity. She had wanted to borrow some stamps; he had asked her if she was all right: "You aren't really well, are you?" *Are* you? Did he see somewhere in her face the shadow of the stones, did he see black spots left behind, little cancerous spores like pits left burned by feet made of acid, what did he see? There on the paper before her, the word, spore; or was it spoor? How cold it was in here, it was hard to see the paper, harder still to hold the pen. I'm fine, she had said; don't call the doctor, I'm fine.

So many doctors; this new one was not bad, he seemed to understand, so many pressures on her and he seemed to understand: work, and the children; the paralytic cold. Of her other difficulties, of her husband and that woman, he was sympathetic, he was not unkind. Again and again he reminded her of her children, of her friends, her mother and brother, the people who cared: like an army of love, massed around her to give her strength. She needed strength, now more than ever; given at times to anger but at heart she was not a fighter; better, perhaps, if she had been. Little girl dreams; and flung stones; it was cold enough to freeze stones in here, sacks of ice split open to show like a pearl the motionless heart.

She had always hated the cold. Little girl days, watching the ocean; the spray like the sparkle of weapons, tips of arrows shining in the sun. Her dead father underground, no light for him. She felt her hand move across the paper, felt the pen as if it were another finger, sweet and special deformity; it was her talent, her genius, it was what allowed her to write. Did everyone have something like that, some rich handicap that in paradox freed its host? Her husband, what was his deformity? A penis that hissed like a snake, a fat red snake with one hot eye? and hers, what was *hers,* patent-leather bitch with her heavy scent and her voice like a man's, what did she have that made her special? Besides him?

Her hand distracting, moving again and she read the line aloud to herself like honey on the tongue: read it again but softly, she did not want to wake the children, wake her neighbor belowstairs; he needed his sleep. She needed sleep, too, but she needed this more.

Black stones, the poem told her, were in essence secret monuments to suffering, scattered across the unforgiving earth as grave markers for sadnesses and sorrows yet to be: and the job of each to find and gather the stones belonging to him, to her, to pile them in a cairn that was itself a monument to the human capacity for self-inflicted pain. And what—pen in hand and in the dark, what is in your pile, what lies in half-completion waiting agonies to be?

The baby made a noise; a car passed outside. Her bladder ached lightly and she stood for a moment, one hand on the chair's back, the other on her own, pressing where the pain seemed to be. So many pains below the surface; so many spots she could not reach. On the chair, draped like mockery the party dress, blue bodice glittering false and sweet; she looked away; she looked down. Sitting in the car, hands in her lap she had been sitting in the car and suddenly there was her neighbor, knocking on the window, was she all right? People were always asking her that; was she? The blue bodice tight as a secret against her heart and she had told him she was fine, then too, just fine; I'm thinking, she had said. I'm going on a nice long holiday, a long rest. She might have said, I'm going off to war; for war you need weapons; perhaps that was in the poem, too, hidden like a snake in the pile of stones. So many stones.

Here a stone for her father's death, dark sugary light surrounding it like infrared; red-eyed and eight years old, she had composed a document for her mother to sign: *I will never marry again.* What a big stone that was, yet unheavy; without trying she could lift it with the bent tip of her nail. Beside it another stone for her mother, a small one shaped like a kidney; and a smaller stone still, for a baby unborn.

More—so many?—for men, most so small her own sad contempt might have goaded her into overlooking them had she not stumbled, stubbed her toes (like her father, in fact, before her, and what were those red marks creeping like unhealed scars up her legs?), understanding like a job begun in the vertiginous moment that these stones too were hers to carry and to keep. In her hands they were not so heavy, though walking in the cold made them more so, the long cold shadow born of the darkness of the biggest stone of all. That one she deliberately sidestepped, big and black as a monument itself, heavy as the weight of his body in the dark; it was, she thought (and said; did she say it aloud?) no longer hers to carry: let *her* carry it instead, the covetous bitch, let her bear the burden now.

Other stones—the *New Yorker* disappointments, the O'Connor class, all of it now as if seen from a painless distance, yet the edges of each stone still shone with a particular and vindictive clarity, as if they had been freshly sharpened not an hour before. Newer rejections (as *he*, the bastard, was basking in light) made their own pile, their own deadly memorial heap and beyond them more, a field of them, a waterless strand: her poverty, her loneliness, even the cold made a carpet of black all the way to the horizon, an endlessness like the tears of the dying, of those who die alone. Despairing of bearing them, she let fall the ones in her arms; there were too many, it was all too much, an army equipped with a pile this big, fierce black edges like excised teeth and the world itself one howling mouth, velvet-dark like the jaws of a guard dog, slick and scentless, dangerously cold.

You could burn to death, in cold like that.

The baby began whimpering in earnest; she rose, back twingeing, to check on him, moving quiet and surely as upon the surface of a lake, frozen water slick and hard as promises, depthless as the edge of the knife, the smile in the darkness, the heavy scent of gas.

Now it was three thirty, quarter to four; she had thought of making coffee, tea, something hot but in the end the poem held her, kept her cramping hands busy. What if—head to one side, sinusitis ache but she was too busy, now, to notice—what if there were a way to make of the stones more than monuments, what if instead they were weapons, but weapons to be used on others rather than self? And take the step, not a long step at all, a logical motion to make of the stones themselves an army, who was it sowed the dragon's teeth? She did not remember, English major, Smith girl, she should remember. Perhaps the poem itself was a stone. Perhaps it was her stone, perhaps she ought to throw it at someone, good and hard, no secret about *that* and she almost laughed; or did she? Did the baby stir? Sweet baby, sometimes it was so hard to look after him, to look after them both; fatherless woman with her fatherless children, alone on a plain of black stones. Set the children down awhile, give them your flesh on which to sleep, to make a carpet keeping them from the cold; she loved her children; it was so hard.

The pen in her hand moved a moment; she ignored it; stubbornly it moved again and the stones shifted, now they were a path, built deliberate and strong for the wheels of iron, the chariots of the queens: warrior queens, and what a grand tradition that was, bare breasts and hair like eagles, their very gazes enough to split a rock, split the boulders in their paths and beside them the men, running, panting, trying to keep up. They knew, those women—with a smile, there was no denying it, a smile there in the sober light— they knew all about war, about tactics and plans, about ways to thwart the enemy even when he lies beside you (and how he lies); they were not fooled, they were not afraid. It was crippling, fear, debilitating as the cold; it was cold, fear, like a stone on your heart. A warrior queen, what would she do? smash the stone, or the heart it breaks? Smash your head open like a stone, and let the cold brain bleed out like jelly through the cracks.

Tired, now, of thinking, the brief exhilaration making her instead ready to weep, like the false gaiety of alcohol, giddy champagne nerves, when had she last drunk champagne? When had she last had reason? To friends she had determinedly crowed in false bravado of her newfound escape from the suffocation of pure domesticity, she was free now, she was doing what she had always wanted to do; her work was tremendous in its new liberation, well that was true, these poems were the best of her life. Her life: what else? Again her thoughts circling, thinking of him, then of her baby boy, a little tyrant too to one woman, one day?—or more, her mouth turning down again, long tragedian's mask but subtle, subtle, she had suffered so long she knew how it was done, without fanfare, without tears if possible, certainly without the long distorting grimace; a pale frown would do as well, as well. What *about* him, this boy-baby, her son? and what about her daughter, plump toddler's cheek and trusting eyes, innocent of the need for weapons, she did not even guess there was a war. How to look at such innocence, both of them, neither of them knew a thing about men and women, love and envy, the way it feels when the black millstone grinds against your heart, the way it feels to breathe blood and call it air. How to keep them safe, how to save herself? how to *understand*, these stones so real she could feel them, feel them in her hands like Medusa's breasts, big, contemptuous, and cold. She put her hands to her face and did not cry, but felt somewhere— in the gripe of her belly, the somber turn of the blood in her womb—the tears, rolling, turning like acid in a vase, the shivering sea undrowned by all the stones in all the world.

And how could she change that?

Finished, now, with the poem; done thinking and her hands loose and empty on the table, pen down and paper folded; she had left a note downstairs, pinned to the hallway pram. No solution but an elegance of decision, there was calm in a decision, a space delicious as the pure moments postfever where the scorched body can relax for a heartbeat's minute before taking up the sterner work of health. She knew what needed to be done, as surely as any warrior queen, sure as the wheels of chariots grinding sparks from the stones below.

Turning on the gas, hand on the dial like the hand of the angel who opens at last the book of life, the silent seeping odor and she bent, half-kneeling, to the door, one toweled hand to steady her motion—she was so tired, up all night and she was so tired—the other past her bending head, bending as if in benediction to slip into growing warmth the metal tray of muffins, breakfast for the children, for herself: hard little pumpernickel muffins like black stones to be heated till they were soft; and warm; and ready. She filled the three mugs with milk; already it was light outside.

The Disquieting Muse

THEY SAT IN A CIRCLE AROUND HIM, in the room as white as a block of salt, as Lot's pale wife turned from defiance to thoughtful critique of humors no less stringent than her own: and they listened; anyway he thought they were listening, sometimes it was hard to tell. Debbie, arms folded, head cocked like a clever pet; Mrs. Wagner who had trouble keeping her mouth closed; Mr. Aronson who would not stay still.

"We're going to work," he said, using his doctor's voice, calm and pleasant, was it pleasant? "in red this time." Red, the tricksy color, blood and guts and resonance all the way back to the womb, like echoes, bread crumbs left to mark the trail of an access forever now denied. Rubbing at his nose, half-unconscious and then consciously stopped, too much like a tic. Daily surrounded by movements deliberate and not, he kept his own affect even, his motions minimal and serene; a berg of calm in this endlessly juddering sea. "Red today, to help us feel our emotions." No one said anything. "Does anyone need any additional materials, any paint? Mrs. Wagner? Debbie? Mr. Aronson, are you going to join us today?"

"Fuck off."

"You know, Mr. Aronson," Debbie's petulance, that false gentility behind clown's eyes, the yellow curve of nail so long it was hard for her to hold a brush, a piece of chalk, a pencil stub, "you know I asked you not to use that word. I mean I asked you not to use that—"

"You fuck off too, lardass."

"Dr. Coles," immediately, lips around the words like food; not enough art therapy in the world to help Debbie, not enough therapy period. "Doctor, I have asked him not to use that word because it's an ugly word, Doctor, and we're here to create beauty, isn't that what we're—"

"Oh for fuck's sake," and Mr. Aronson out of the chair, Mrs. Wagner's big mouth bending in that deep unnerving smile that always made him think of animals, big wet animals down in the mud, look at the slouch of those breasts, big breasts, her back must be killing her. Something wet, not paint, across her dirty blouse, red and gold windmills and Debbie was still going on about beauty, beauty and Mr. Aronson grabbed his crotch and said, "You make me sick right here, you know it? You and your fucking beauty," and behind his own eyes, his careful noncommittal frown he felt nothing; not even annoyance; nothing at all.

"Dr. Coles!"

Like voices from a painting; he had been an art major. Last night Margaret had asked him about *Guernica*, did it feel like *Guernica* every day, did it feel like Bacon or Bosch? No, trying for lightness, no it feels like a painting of a clown. Her smile against his neck, reaching around to feel for his cock; her fingers were always so cold, cold now and "Black velvet," she said, "a black velvet clown." The head of his cock was red, a royal color against the elegant bleach of her hands, her red nails, red as the paint they were using today and now Mr. Aronson had consented to sit, Debbie was still talking but Mr. Aronson had consented to sit and Mrs. Wagner was smiling now down at the colors, red on the floor and between her knees and red on the backs of her hands.

It took him a minute to realize it was not paint.
Sometimes it was *Guernica,* after all.

He went for a drink, wanting to call Margaret, not wanting
to stay in his office long enough to make the call; more
than usually tired, of course it had been an ugly day. He
had three drinks almost before he noticed, three small
squat glasses of scotch; he did not like scotch, hard liquor,
secretly preferring fruity drinks, rum and pink froth but he
felt like an asshole ordering them here, anywhere, wanting
Margaret to order one first so he could say I'll try that too,
what is it? Knowing what it was. Margaret knew he knew,
too, but didn't care, or said she didn't; Margaret said he
should drink what he wanted.

He was rubbing his nose again, made himself stop again
and then suddenly angry rubbed hard, faint oil beneath his
fingers and he could rub his own fucking nose, couldn't he?
Tics; shit. You make me sick right here. He left the fourth
glass untouched; a headache and he went home, the message light on and Margaret's voice, sweet, light as pink froth
saying I can't come tonight, there's a meeting, marketing
and so on and on, he closed his eyes halfway through. Her
voice; her white fingers on his cock. His erection was flabby
and small, tired. It had taken over an hour to clean the room
after what Mrs. Wagner had done. At least she was out of the
group now, back to the wards, sixty days minimum like a
reward; maybe it was. It was for him, anyway.

Among his colleagues he was unique; and always
uncomfortable, did they know, could they smell it on him?
Art therapist, but forever more art than therapy; he had
never had grand plans, saving the world, saving the sick
from themselves, Art's white knight with the key to free
expression in his warm collegiate hand. He had been an art

major first, but so unconnected, so thoroughly lost amid the rush and thickets of images caught and captured—too large for him, he knew it the way the ant fears the spider and his advisor had recommended a change in venue.

But I love art, he had said. You can love it there too, the advisor said, you can help other people love it; and then there was a link, a proven bridge between creativity and, say it, madness. Craziness. The crazies always get there first, his instructor used to say; listen to them. Jeremy, listen: her gaze on his, big Teutonic blonde with a handshake that could crush rocks. You've got to learn to listen.

His own aptitude had surprised him; his first client had been an even bigger surprise, noisy and stinky, he would never forget her smell if he lived to be a hundred. Piss smell, people said, Margaret when he told her the story. They don't wash, they pee themselves. But it wasn't that, he couldn't explain, it was something cellular, something to do with the way her eyes had rolled in her head, rolled like a horse's eyes, the way her fingers closed around the stem of the brush as if she held the tube of his windpipe in that moist considering grasp, he could hardly breathe, he could hardly wait until it was over.

But she made progress, that woman, her psychologist had told him so. Cornering him outside the therapy room, glorified holding tank but "It's really incredible," smiling, "she's finally coming along. You really opened her up," and he, small Judas smile of incomprehension both utter and dire; the curse of luck: oh God I am good at this, oh God. A roomful of newsprint paintings in wet blues and stinky blacks, she talks, it's terrific; oh God.

Two years past and he was still helping them, luck's blind hand in his own, unsure how someone like Mr. Aronson, say, or fucked-up Mrs. Wagner could take anything from what he gave, or rather lay out for the taking: there was, he thought, no active sense of giving, he put the tools before them, they had to want to be helped. To change. To use art itself as a catalyst for self-expression and through self-expression find the freedom to free themselves; he told all this to Margaret and she laughed, head on his chest and she laughed, her fingers curled loose about his own.

"You sound like a course description," she said, "a brochure," but she was smiling, holding his hand and smiling and he smiled back at her. What did she know, she wasn't there, she had no idea. Clean Margaret with her hands cold as a clinician, cold as the hands of the clock. He had not told her, finally, of Mrs. Wagner, fresh new sense of failure, of luck denied; but now, two days later and Long John was grabbing him in the hall, like a principal collaring a tardy student: "Nice fucking work, Jer. Nice fucking piece of work."

Staring at him but not straight on, six feet four and yardstick arms even longer in that white coat, dirty collar, it smelled faintly of sweat. And gravy, cafeteria gravy. Is he happy? Is he angry? Nice piece of work, Jer. "I don't—"

"Mrs. Wagner, you know, Mrs. Out-to-Lunch? Cut herself up in your playroom, you know. Anyway today's my day with her and out it comes, big problems, she hates her husband, she hates her kids. Hates everybody, me, you, herself for putting up with it. Mad, and screaming like hell. She's ready to talk, now."

"That's—I didn't know, that's really—"

"Maybe I ought to invest in some crayons, huh. Lucky you," and gone, still smiling and he left behind to adjust for himself a smile, he had done it again; how? Mrs. Out-to-Lunch; blood on her hands and his hands in his pockets, white coat clean as a piece of new paper, as an unmade wish and in the end what difference did it make, she was

Long John's problem now and they would be sending him a new one, another one to take her place. Maybe today, maybe next session, what difference did it make?

That evening Debbie cried, and Mr. Aronson called her a lardass and drew a picture of a big black bird pecking out her eyes before relenting enough to admire her drawing of a box of chocolates and a sweetheart bow, she was really a terrific draftsman, Debbie; the bow looked completely real, down to the dust in its creases; it was an old box of chocolates, she said. He himself sketched loops and circles, long lines, geometries in spiral like fractals split down their bloodless middles and left to dry in logic's light, and Mr. Aronson squinted over his shoulder and said, "Hey Debbie, look at this—he can't draw."

That evening Margaret came to him, soft smile and a half-drunk bottle of margarita mix; her panties were as pink and shiny as her vulva, but it took him almost half an hour to come. She said, still smiling, that it didn't matter; she did not stay the night.

Her name was Ruth, and she smelled like all the others only more so; like milk and cloudy water, like some fish caught dying in a frozen lake. Albino eyes and a file made heavy with page after page of recommendations, half-sure diagnoses like a map of a land unseen. At the bottom someone had written Schizoaffective? in heavy red ink; it was crossed out in black, the pen strokes light and thin as hairs.

She would not sit by Mr. Aronson; Debbie went not ignored so much as unnoticed, it was as if she did not actually see Debbie at all. Bare white arms crossed across the hospital gown; the chart said she refused to wear street clothes, underclothes. Her hair was incredibly dirty, a thin and gummy blonde. When he tried to speak to her she ignored him too, so he turned instead to the others, told them they would be working in pencil again today, told them to express what they felt to be their worst conflict this week, whether with the staff, or other clients, or themselves.

"How about you?" Mr. Aronson said. "What if it's with you?"

"Then express it," half-listening; he was watching her, was she going to ignore this, too? But no, she had pencil in hand, bent so close to the paper her dirty hair brushed it, was she nearsighted? Perhaps she had broken or lost her glasses, perhaps they had been stolen, it happened all the time. Short definite strokes, the pencil wearing down; sharpened but not sharp, he had learned not to make them too sharp. Mr. Aronson was complaining about the light so he turned on all the overheads, grainy fluorescence, it made her look more pasty-green than ever. At the end of the hour Debbie and Mr. Aronson had expressed their conflicts with the staff, both over the issue of smoking in the dayroom; Ruth was still working, but set the pencil aside as he approached.

"Ruth?" pleasantly, he always tried to be pleasant. God did she smell. Leaning over her shoulder, careful not to touch, to see centered on the page before her a correct and detailed drawing of a large flayed penis, spread like a flower, delicately pinned.

"It's a horse cock," she said. "I hope you like it."

That night he read through her file again, sure and slow like a man wading through a swamp. No firm diagnosis, neuroleptics had been tried without result. No auditory hallucinations, although a psychologist at Busey had speculated she might be hebephrenic; she had been hospitalized here for three months, had done poorly since admittance, at least they could all agree on that. One of the attendants had found her drawing with lit cigarettes on the grey linoleum of the dayroom floor, and so they had sent her to him.

Debbie did not like her, nor did Mr. Aronson; they both seemed if not afraid then studiously wary, careful to keep their distance. They sat almost together, chairs an inch from touching, as Ruth in grimy isolation dipped her brush like a sixth finger, one heavy spot of blue acrylic shiny as a bruise on her white knee. Through the soiled drift of her gown he could see, if he looked, the firm shapes of her breasts, conical breasts bigger, say, than was proportionate, bigger than Margaret's.

If he looked.

He knew he wanted to look, he wanted to see: past the dirty hair and smelly skin, track where the attraction lay: for there was attraction, he was honest enough, bewildered enough to admit it.

Why?

Her silence was peculiar, not the leaden quiet of depression nor the blank affect of incipient catatonia; it was not anhedonia, for she was capable of pleasure: she enjoyed her food, according to the file. Did she enjoy her art therapy? who knew? She did not yell like Mr. Aronson, or bitch like Debbie; she rarely volunteered remarks. Once or twice he thought he had caught her looking at him, a gaze studied and cold as a reptile's; but nothing she did seemed to indicate that she gave him more notice than the chair she sat on, the easel she used to paint.

She had been with him nearly a month now, once a week her drawings, paintings and always one a session, never less or more: after the horse penis (and what fun he had had logging that in his notes) came a headless female torso covered in slit-pupiled eyes, its hands fisted and firm on the lapping head of the male figure between its legs; a pair of three-armed women locked in some strange hybrid of combat and sex; a blindfolded prepubescent girl about to penetrate herself with what looked like a broken baseball bat—she had titled that one, calling it *The Dream of Reason*. Did she dream? She would not say, would not answer when to draw her out he talked of his own dreams, lightly, lying; in reality they were simple sex-dreams, fantasies made figment in the empty sweaty dark, but lately in waking it was as if her drawings, or their shadows, lay caul-like across the innards of his eyes; he had to sit up in bed, turn on the light like a child in a nightmare, ignoring his erection the way you ignore the unpleasant, a street person on the corner, a dead animal splashed on your turning wheels.

He had made photocopies of the drawings for his files; alone in the bedlamp light he now took them out, feeling absurdly like a boy with a girlie magazine; remembering, like a book read, his first time masturbating to *Penthouse*, he had come all over the magazine, his brother's magazine and his brother had teased him, but kindly, he was in the fraternity now. Drawings in his hand, wondering again how to reconcile that vast technique with the impenetrable fact of her silent physical self, the sloppy swing of her breasts beneath the gown; how to interpret the power of those images, their brute sexuality; their affect on him.

But it was natural, wasn't it, to be affected, they would affect any man, they were so detailed, so frankly sexual and she was so very sick

So very sick and helpless.

He slept with the drawings spread across him like limbs; and woke to dreams of nothing that morning could recall.

Today it was acrylics again, Mr. Aronson vocal about his dislike for painting, Debbie listless with blues and purples and off in her corner Ruth, hands in constant motion, her blank face still. He found within himself a kind of new impatience, a wish for the others somehow to be still, to be gone; it was Ruth he wanted to study, Ruth he wanted to see. Standing silent beside her in the surrounding atmosphere of her smell, it was like standing next to a statue for all the interest she displayed, bending close now to see better and suddenly she turned, turned on him in complete distilled awareness and he, stepping back in almost comical alarm brushed with the back of one moving hand the side of her breast, half-visible, big and white beneath the gown.

He said nothing, did not apologize, at once beside Debbie and her sloppy cornflowers and he was hard, shamefully hard, he could not look at Ruth again. Discussing at length Mr. Aronson's work, Debbie's, the session was nearly over when he went at last and slowly to her side.

The paper was full, dire blue background bisected by a pair of Byzantine highways, intricate and red, both dead-ending in a grim little house with broken windows; beneath, in her stylized printing, she had lettered *Margaret's Fallopian Tubes*. He felt her watch him read the words, her gaze all arctic composure, her slippered feet crossed lightly at the ankles like a duchess at a drawing-room tea; when he asked her (still hard; oh God that smell) some standard questions she ignored him as thoroughly as before.

He omitted the name's coincidence in his notes, in his conscious thoughts but making love to Margaret in the night's dry-furnace air the image found him, red roads like snakes, like wires, like vast veins feeding and writhing and between the veins the image of Ruth unbidden, pulling up her dirty gown to show him, oh show me and "What are you doing," her sweet voice blurry, now, raising up on her elbows, "Jeremy, what are you doing?" and looking down between them saw like a peep show stranger the tilted gush of his orgasm on her belly and her thighs.

"I don't know," and then in a rush, as if in waking, "Oh God I'm sorry, Margaret, I'm sorry," but she was sliding out from under him, she was wiping herself with his shirt, expensive green linen but he said nothing, she was angry, she had a right to be. She stayed the night but slept cocooned, her back to him as smooth and martial as a blade exposed. In the morning she smiled, but evaded his kisses; I'll call you, she said. Not tomorrow, but soon.

He had a day off coming; he took it, spent it like a sentence served at home with her file. Page after page, it was as if he could smell her there, her dirty skin, her drawings between them like challenge and tease. He was not helping her; she would not speak, perform simple tasks of hygiene; in her psychotherapy she was if not actually regressing then certainly making no progress at all. Perhaps he should ask for a change, to have her transferred out. But if he did they would want to know why, they would ask for an explanation and instantly, absurdly the defense, a guilty anger: I haven't even *done* anything, I haven't even touched

oh yes you have

and angrier still, shoving the file away; he was doing the best he could, all that he could. He would give it another month, and if he had had no luck by then he would ask for a change; he would tell them it was in her best interests, it was best for both of them, it was the best he could do.

The white room abysmally cold, and emptier by one: Mr. Aronson had pneumonia again, his smoker's lungs invaded, exacerbated by the daily failures of the heat. In Mr.

Aronson's absence Debbie was tearful and hard to handle, she kept accusing him of complicity with her mother, of taking phone calls from her mother behind her back. In her drawings she caricatured him as the devil, fat strokes, big goatish hooves; still weeping she left early, fleeing to rec therapy, leaving him alone with Ruth.

Who did not seem to notice the cold, still in her gown, same gown, same steady hand on the pencil. His promises, his firm inner precepts now seemed less stringent, less worthy of resolve in this moment of watching her, greasy hair and the sway of her breasts as her arms moved, he was watching her, doing nothing but watching her: busy hands now choosing among the pencils, new pencils, and he seeing as if in a light removed the fact of her absolute availability, yes call it helplessness, call it sickness spread and gleaming and her hands now on the thick stems of the pencils, black graphite shine down the planes of her thighs. "I'm drawing my veins," she said, quiet in the quiet around her, turned to face him and he saw spit on her lips, "I'm drawing how it *goes*," and as loose and careless her hands to pull aside entirely the gown, show herself, spread herself with the pencils in a grotesquerie acrobatic, it reminded him of the laboratory, pins, an anatomical drawing and he was so hard it hurt, ached like skin pulled to bursting and she saw or seemed to see because she smiled, smiled straight into his eyes as she slipped one pencil deep inside her; and pulled it out to sign her name across the bottom of her paper.

And left; and he behind, moving to pick up the pencil by its dry eraser tip and hold it, close to his nose and breathe; his hands were shaking, he felt as if he was going to come, to be sick, both. Closing his eyes to open them to the drawing, lines and shading and this time she had drawn herself, head back and naked, raised legs like a whore's and past her spreading fingers the fact of eyes, staring out from her darkness, staring at him.

Drawing and pencil wrapped in two quick motions, stuffing them both in his case and he was pulling on his gloves, his hands were shaking and shaking as he drove, home and the house warm around him as he took the drawing to the bathroom and masturbated, crying out as he came, no name, no sound, nothing more human than the whuff of air back in lungs tight as Mr. Aronson's, strangled tight and over his breathing he heard Margaret's voice on the machine, cool and sweet and distant as a face in a magazine.

He took another day off, a personal day; he was sick, he said, lying, maybe he had caught Aronson's bug. Dry cough like a phony adulterer, hanging up to stretch back down, shirt and tie, he had tried to get up, to go; but could not go. Not today. You're the doctor, aren't you? Aren't you? Shaking his head in the blind-drawn light, no; no to what? He was trying his best, wasn't he; or was he, subtly, in ways he did not recognize, encouraging those drawings, that illness, using strategies that on the surface were both rational and defensible but when viewed another way, turned right-side up, were nothing but yet another narrowing and easing of the way, the way *in,* the one path and the hunger thoughtless as a rock, a cock, his own hard cock like a breathing animal; using his power to help instead to damage and damage ineffably, brutally, fierce infection of desire meeting head-on the infection of her illness; and she was very ill, there was no question of that, no question at all.

Confusion like a migraine, his hands damp on his temples; he had seen patients sit this way and in that thought stopped at once; stop it. It all had to stop. He had to make a change; he must admit he could not help her. Notes on the back of other notes, structuring a memo, discontinue art therapy. Why? Because I want to fuck her, that's why, because fucking her is not in her best interests. The memo written he felt somehow easier, he would hand it in tomorrow, he would be grave and composed. She could switch over to rec therapy—bouncing in her gown, that cold empty face and legs spread in calisthenics, oh God let it not be his problem, I never wanted to do this and he was talking out loud, talking to the drawing of Ruth, the eyes that seemed to see him even more clearly here, in his home, in his room, see and know more clearly than he the wet clarity of his wants: the dirty, the bad, the wrong and infinitely wrongful, the stink of the toilet in his nose and every time he saw her it was as if he committed anew some warm atrocity, her slack passivity a goad and her hand between her legs, the clenched drawing like kissing dry lips and his belt undone and jingling absurd as spurs, he was going to come, here and now and in frantic haste he pushed the drawing against his body, her penciled legs open, gluey and sticky and the angle was wrong, all wrong and oh God it was already over, down his legs the river translucent as a stream of cloudy tears, heat turned cold in an instant and he was breathing like a horse, like a beaten animal

and she was there

there in the room, wearing her gown, smiling beneath those cold white eyes. Tangled hair and gritty feet, her slippers a color like dirt against the muted blue plush of the carpeting, her edges hyperreal and clear as a drawing; he could even smell her, that milky musky stink like an animal in estrous. It was like the hallucinations his patients reported: so real they couldn't be real.

"I'm your charm," she said, her grin in his face, hands beneath her breasts in proffering pose, black parody of a stripper, of a dancer in a bar. "I'm your *luck*. You didn't think you could do all this without luck, did you? You didn't think that, did you?"

He was breathing so hard his chest hurt, his lungs beneath the bone as strictured as ligaments, as muscles torn and he could not stop, breathing as loud as some misfunctioning machine. His cock had shrunk to a limp purplish smallness, as if it too were a muscle now deprived of strength; the semen was cold. His arms against the bedclothes trembled, as if he were really ill.

"Because there's nothing warm in you," her voice so calm, pleasant as his own when he addressed a crying Debbie, a raving Mr. Aronson, bleeding Mrs. Wagner and all of them, all of them, her hands like spiders at her sides. "Nothing warm at all but the place for luck, and that's *me*," really pleased now, really smiling. "That's me."

Closer, her hair a special gray with grease collected and it was past imagining but he was getting an erection, she was close enough to touch and "I'm your charm," she said again, "your lucky star," and with one contemptuous hand reached to squeeze his cock, her hand as big as his own, squeeze it to the cusp of pain and he said her name, Ruth, said it once and twice, Ruth, head down and eyes as empty as any patient's, RUTH and she squeezed him harder, RUTH and she squeezed him again.

Margaret left four unanswered messages on his machine before she stopped calling entirely.

Queen of Angels

IN THE WATER-GREEN HALF-LIGHT his lips protrude, moist starlet red, glossy and swollen as sweet infection; his irises are grey. When she touches him, he makes no sound at all; but his lips move.

He might be praying; or trying to speak.

He never says her name.

Down the hall again; still. Just after nine on the heavy clock, white face in dust behind bland mesh and big black numbers you could see from either end of the hall; the all-purpose institutional clock. Hospitals and schools. And prisons. And nursing homes. Walking, her back threatening to lock, that feeling again like grinding bones in sockets scraped dry and she leaned for a moment against the wall. Tired inside and out, calf muscles cramping like they had all day; every day; she was so tired of working here. Continuing care; right. Tired of bending over, of the smells and the way shit feels between your fingers, you're wearing gloves but that doesn't really help, does it? The endless rosary of pills, meds twice a shift and she was tired of that, too. Tylenol and vitamins, and Darvocett. And Xanax. She wished she could have some Xanax. In the room closest to her, Mrs. Reichert was screaming again. Pretty soon they would all be screaming.

She was so tired of hearing people scream.

She had been here for four years, but they were all still

people to her; helpless. Most of the aides called them by their illnesses, their ailments, walking tragedies: the Parkinson's, the CVAs, the Alzheimer's; a whole family's worth of Alzheimer's. Strokes and dementia, congestive heart failure.

Her name was Deborah, but he never said her name.

The first time she saw him he was wrapped like a pupa, mummy in white bony and incongruous, shivering mute with some vast disturbance; he could not talk; his family talked too quietly and at such length that she could not stop to listen; she had work to do. Count meds, her fat shifting pile of paperwork, charting BMs and electrolyte counts, blood and urine, all the fluids rich and thin; a whole future in a plastic sample container: I can tell you where you'll be in a year, six months; six weeks.

The family was in a hurry, despite the time they spent talking; she saw them go. None of them said goodbye to their—what? Husband? Brother? Little brother. He was barely forty, she saw: Elliot. His name was Elliot and he had had a stroke, a cardiovascular accident. Some accident. With good care he would live a long time, but he would never know a minute of it.

—Would he? Did they know, the ones whose brains took disaster's brunt while leaving their bodies intact, slow wreck of blood and shoaling bone, endlessness replicated with each breath, each intubation? The nurses and aides debated this, when they had time, a few minutes with coffee or a Coke, one of the aides dropping ashes on his shoes; sneakers. She wore sneakers, too. She used to wear regular nurse's shoes but found she liked sneakers better, sometimes she had to move very fast and the crepe soles had slowed her down.

"Does he even know he's in there, that's what I wonder."

The aide dropped ashes again. "I mean, *look* at him. Look at any of 'em."

She shrugged. The other nurse sipped coffee, cursed softly for a scalded lip; shook her head. "They're not there anymore, no way. They're just empty bottles." The image seemed to please her; she said it again. "Empty bottles," and when Deborah shrugged again, "Come on, Deb. You know that."

"I don't know anything." Her back locked again in half a motion, dry pestle grind. The aide put out his cigarette. "Hey Deb," the other nurse said. She had a jaundiced bruise shaped heavy as a thumb print above her left eyebrow. "You really believe that? That they can hear us, they know what's going on?"

No. I don't know. "I don't know what I believe."

"If it ever happens to me," quick paper squeeze between strong fingers, tossing her empty cup in the trash, "I know what I want and fuck my family. No code, no way."

"Get a MedAlert bracelet," Deborah said. "'Slow code.'"

Full code meant resuscitate; no code meant what it said. All the patients wanted was a way out, but sometimes the families were obdurate: do everything possible, they said. Guilt and rage and terror, as if keeping them alive meant anything anymore; rag talismans, strapped and bleeding and feeding from tubes, tubes for food and tubes for shit and someone's daughter, someone's niece, someone's grandson shaking their heads: bring her back, they said. If anything happens, bring him back. Slow code was the compromise, the last mercy unspoken: stop for a drink of water, stop to check your watch. Inside the room the decision is in progress, relentless as the process of birth. We did everything we could; and it is a fact, like oxygen: it is simply the truth.

Elliot was a no-code.

Nothing was too likely to happen to Elliot, though; except for an essentially empty head he was in pretty good shape. Waxy as a still Pieta Christ, long muscles in the cheap cleanser-blue pajamas and less trouble than a potted plant; the smell from his body was warm, the way a baby is warm, damp smooth skin against a sheltering cheek. Deborah's notes on his chart were routine. She never wrote down the way he smelled, the peculiar oval shape of his lips as if steeped in a pleasing dream. He never screamed, cried; cried out. No one ever came to see him.

Which in its way was good. Immersed in permanent solitude, he missed no one; unlike some of the others, the daily pitiful litany: where is my husband? Where is June, my daughter June? Is Michael here? A very few of them had families who came every day, to nurse their own, each deadening chore made sacred by abundant martyring love. To feed, coax with homemade delicacies mouths too slack to chew; to wash them, to change their laundry, soft pastel percale, bright flowers. To read to them, to talk. It was sadder that way, hideous the families' suffering, but it made Deborah feel obscurely better. The ones she hated to see were the ones who came once a year, hectic with their own agenda, guilt and loathing vivid as a blood trail and full of complaints and rages for the staff: perhaps the patient has not had her diaper changed this hour; perhaps the patient's hair has not yet been washed. They explode as if finding vivisection in process, curse and call names, last month a man poked Deborah in the name badge, stiff finger so hard the thin plastic edge eased like a needle through her uniform and into her skin.

"I don't," poking, "want to see my mother like this. *Ever.* Do you understand me?"

Go fuck yourself. "What's the matter?" leaning a little

away from him, his pointing finger, his bitter cigarette breath. His mother was Mrs. White, Susanna: another CVA, victim of a carotid artery angioplasty that loosed a clot unseen like death itself come claiming through her veins. Quad and trach and tube feed and oxygen, that was Susanna. She had two daughters living three thousand miles away, and a son close enough for daily visits. It was two days after Christmas, his annual appearance and he poked Deborah again.

"She *smells*," he said.

"We'll take care of it," Deborah said.

"Don't patronize me," he said. "I'm paying for all this."

And heaven too. "We'll take care of it," she said, in the tone of voice she sometimes used when a patient was particularly hysterical, an iron gentility that usually worked on some level and it was working now, the man was turning away, pulling on his coat; expensive coat. After he had gone she went into Susanna's room and stood beside her for a moment. In the room a faint antiseptic smell, less offensive than an open container of Vick's. Susanna's closed eyes were lidded in layers, like sand dunes, like snow drifts. Deborah felt tired, exquisitely tired, exquisitely sorrowful; but did not cry. Sometimes the patients cried, when the pain got too bad. "Kill me, Debbie." That's what they said. Kill me, Debbie, oh Debbie let me die.

"I can't do that," she would say. "That's not what I'm here for." Then she would go home and vomit; or sit in a chair without moving, without taking off her coat or shoes, a peculiar red illness moving like a secret snake through stomach and lungs as if her body itself were crying, tears of slow and heavy blood.

Elliot never cried. Or moved. Or spoke. Elliot's muscles were holding up surprisingly well, he was not withering as quickly as expected. The first time his eyes came open, Deborah immediately beeped his doctor; who upon inspection informed her that what she had reported had not happened.

Nothing there, pale grey as winter water frozen in the last moment of motion. Drowning Elliot, slender bony chin, sarcophagus profile and her stethoscope brushed against his chest as now she bent, back painful, to adjust the slender slope of a tube and his eyes did not move and from his lips extruded a delicate drop of matter as fragile as a pearl, that rolled across his cheek to lie like an angel's tear on the black-stamped linen of his bed.

She picked it up.

There in the baggy pocket of her clinician's coat and her hand kept moving to touch it, roll it between nervous fingers, she had checked him twice as often as necessary through her shift but there was no change, no others like it lying beside him, Elliot inert, winter windows gray with the breath of others; it was a creamy color, hard as bone. Maybe it was bone.

She checked him once more before leaving; the pillows, the linen beside him was bare. His lips looked slightly sore, as if chapped by the wind. His vitals were OK. "Elliot," she said, not to him.

His mouth moved, lips pursing almost like a kiss, an exaggerated Hollywood kiss; but nothing came out, nothing she could see. Her hands shook as she bent to the pillow, the face upon it calm as a dead saint; his eyes did not open, but moved, slow, slow, beneath the shelter of his lids, back and forth like thoughts, the nature of rumination, the play of muscles whose services are by time made moot.

"Elliot?" she said again; to him; a question.

In the hall the sound of the midnight shift, the aides talking quietly to one another; the pearl was in her hand as she left the room.

Instead of sleeping she sat up, the pearl before her on the kitchen table, a space pushed clear of half-empty cereal boxes and Sanka jars and a napkin holder shaped like a triangle. She looked at it dry-eyed in the wash of overhead light. It was not bone; it was not a tooth, or part of one. It was not a gallstone, or kidney stone; it was not a real pearl. She had an impulse to cut it in half, scrape its surface with a nail file but in the end did not, left it whole, left it there on the table on a pale paper napkin and when she slept at last dreamed thinly; not of it or Elliot but of walking forever on a helix still and dusty, no feeling at all but the silent grind of sand beneath her feet.

According to his chart, in two shifts' time Elliot had not produced anything other than some unexceptional urine, but the rest of the last shift had been busy: Hakim Richardson had had another stroke and was sent to the hospital; Mr. Zelinksi died. Mary Yost had escaped her restraints and ate half an Efferdent before she was caught. This brought on some reminiscences of a former patient, an Alzheimer's who ate soap, slim motel-sized bars of Ivory; she would not touch another kind.

"Ivory was her brand," the day nurse supervisor said, smiling as if at the antics of a particularly precocious child, or a clever pet.

"Maybe she liked the taste," Deborah said. She was irritable with lack of sleep, her eyes as sticky-dry as the bottoms of her shoes; she had stepped in something on her way down the hall, back from Elliot's room. Today he seemed paler; his closed eyes did not move at all. His hair looked dirty. There was nothing on the pillow or sheets but she lingered, wanting somehow not to touch but to reach; to connect.

Screams from down the hall; someone hollered "*Deb!*" and she ran, stethoscope banging back against her chest, pounding dull and painful like a little metal heart.

By the time she gave report to the midnight shift it was 11:30; there were still narcotics to count, she had to finish up charting but: stopped, inevitable, before Elliot's door, tired now, and ready to concede it as sheer strangeness, to reaffirm her correct decision not to chart the pearl, any of it; to tell no one.

Inside, a distinct smell; not one she knew.

Her heart felt strange, tight in her body like an over-developed muscle and she approached Elliot as if he might spring up; already she saw his eyes, closed and restless back and forth and then a soundless string like bubbles, spit bubbles and there were at least a dozen of them, popping from between his lips to roll on a snail's path of drool down to the wet square between pillow and blue shoulder, thirteen, fifteen; she swept them all into her cupping hand, hot and wet and her hands were shaking hard enough to be clumsy, she thought she might have dropped one of the pearls but now he had stopped producing them, nothing there but saliva and closed lips.

His eyes had stopped moving.

"Elliot," whispering, the air between her lips warm with that smell, "Elliot." Urgent. "What do you want?"

Nothing.

She had to count the narcotics twice to make them add

up correctly; her hands so awkward the other nurse noticed, asked if she were all right. "Fine," lying, what a poor liar she was. "Just tired." The pearls made a wet square in her pocket, visible moisture; did anyone see? She almost ran a red light going home, stumbled in the kitchen and scraped her shin against the bare leg of a chair. There were too many pearls to fit on the napkin so she hunted up a little jar, little glass cosmetic jar long bare of whatever sweet cream folly it had held; still trapped inside the faint emollient smell. The pearls lay three deep, nestled in the smell, matte against the glass and she took them with her to the bedroom, set them square on the scarred night stand so she could lie on one elbow and consider them: light on, eyes open. There were seventeen; she counted them twice and firmly; seventeen pearls that were not pearls, Elliot's extrusions, Elliot's, what? Voice? Words; pearls of wisdom and she smiled a little but without true humor, there was nothing funny here, there was nothing that she understood. Maybe you had to be like he was to understand; maybe you had to be locked like a boat stuck in ice, like a bricked-in pet, a fetus bobbing endlessly in faint formaldehyde against a jar just like this one, here in her hand filled with pearls that as she watched turned from pale to pink, to dark pink, to red, heavy red and then almost brown; like menstrual blood. Like the surface of a fresh scab. Like an insect crushed juicy and left to dry, mummy-dark on the plane of a screen.

She did not know whether to scream or drop the jar, or call and see if something had happened to Elliot, or empty the pearls down the toilet and pretend she had never seen anything. In the end she did nothing, and in that elongation found sleep to be a long nod, waking to instant consciousness with the pearls primly jarred beside her, safe and snug and surely there.

The day shift nurse's report, hurrying through the patient list till his name, leaping out—and beside it, no change. Nothing.

"How was it?" not so much casual as flat, peripheral gaze. "Anything interesting?" Anybody extrude anything, you know, pearls? No?

"Same old same old." The day nurse supervisor, purse in hand. "You're short-handed today, looks like. David called in sick just a little bit ago."

She shrugged; felt as if there were wires pulling her down the hall, thin almost invisible flesh-colored wires. "Have a good one," the day nurse said.

Elliot's room smelled of nothing, dust, furnace exhalation. His sheets had not been changed: she could see the faint indentation, pattern of wetness dried where the pearls had been. He lay very still as always but informed somehow by a new—weariness? Can one be weary who never moves? Exhaustion, then, say, or say weakness and see its signs: around his lips faint brackets, wrinkles: deeper around the eyes, forever closed in sockets bruised and plummy as an old man's, the skin there softer, soft as the skin of his lips unmarred by blisters, by fluid—by pearls.

"*Deb.*"

Crossly, and her own huge startle; from the doorway, leaning in: "What're you doing? Come on, we need to get going." The other nurse, bruise above her eye now a fruity green; harassed already. "Did you know that asshole David called in sick? Again?"

Down the hall; grinding spine and the tug of wires and it stayed that way all day, even the patients seemed worse, fractious, shrieking, there were fights and falls and everything, showers, meals, meds, running late; she did not see Elliot again but did not cease to feel the wires. A headache began about ten, heavy, thick behind the curve of her fore-head like beating blood; three Tylenols with a grimace of cold coffee and as she swallowed thought, Did Elliot feel it, when the pearls came out? did they hurt?

Did he know she was there?

Troubled dreams; the headache was there when she woke; the pearls were still that deep blood-rusted red. A bad day, bad week; the pearls stayed dark but no new ones came; his fragility increased but no one seemed to see. Her day off came without relief; she had copied his records and spent the day going through them, going through the literature to see if there was anything she might begin to lean on, learn, understanding's crutch but then her disgust and weakness harsh as pain, she pushed the books and charts away and took up the jar: reliquary, was that the name? The resting place for relics, saint's bones, last drops of holy blood; in the light the pearls lay smooth, gentle distortion against the glass and she wept, finally, slow tears that ran against her cheeks, crying with her mouth open dull as a cow's and hands palms-up and flat against her legs like a postulant's prayer, the confession of a man on his deathbed, a voice without inflection imbued with flat and terrible haste.

His weakness accelerated, deeper the weights that held him, the hands that pulled him down: death's hands, death's fingers slipping like thread through the skin of his silence, weaving like strands through the hair brushed clean and flat against his quiet forehead. And she watch-ing, knowing: It was the making of the pearls that caused this deterioration; but how to chart that? how to explain without evidence: show, tell, see? How? Unable to spend time beside him, still she checked, quick, compulsive, watching for eye movement, the telltale drop of pearls; the deepening weakness like a road leading only one way. No one caught her, or rather she caught no one watching; but they were curious, or would be; one day they would ask.

Let them. Stubborn, she would not stop; she had to know. Watching him and tired, more headaches, the pain in her back and snapping at the aides, she did not make mistakes with the patients but neither was she kind; and regretted it, riding home and she wept at a red light and wished for the first time that Elliot would stop, just stop.

Die?

No.

When she got home she saw that all the pearls had turned black.

The next day she tried her best, pathetic avoidance of his room, tried to leave his maintenance to others, tried to do her job and only her job. Not to worry; not to participate; not to understand but only to work and if he wanted to spit pearls then let someone else find them, oh, someone who would call out, "Hey *Deb!*" and show them to her, warm and slick in the rubber valley of a palm amazed and What do you make of this? And she would shrug.

He had lost more weight; he lay like paper in the bed, like some cunning wasp's construction of what a human being might be, spun grey and weightless: death's cocoon and no, instantly, her denial: No.

This morning, checking the pearls, she saw that one of them had deteriorated, turned seemingly to dust, or ash; human ash, gray talcum against the side of the jar.

Dark, clean sheets and on the bed beside him, only watching as his eyes beneath their lids began to move, back and forth like fish in elemental motion, back and forth and the instant bubble of pearls, two, three, a handful. Watching, heart beating breathless and she had a wild desire, in the shadow of those moving eyes, to eat one and raising it to her lips, her shaking hands and inside her mouth, warm, warm on her flat tongue, against her palate like a special stone and she spat it out, gently into her palm that closed instinctively around it like petals concealing the flower's heart. His hand, inert in its place, seemed nonetheless to touch hers; one finger crooked closer than the rest, heaven's rebus and she swept the rest of the pearls into her pocket, rose clumsy and at once at voices in the hall; she almost forgot her purse, there on the floor, tucked under the bed like a visiting friend. Out of the room like a criminal but she did not feel bad, or sad, felt instead the intense absorption she had felt once, when? Long time, her premed courses and learning, slow, the mystery of the body, its failures and desires too stringent to be less than exigencies, less comprehendible as logic than commands from spirit to flesh, less truly understandable than the nature of life; and entropy, death's sweeter sister, hand in hand in decay's pavane begun as soon as birth. The way organs rot, and breathing slows, the way wrinkles and scar tissue form.

The way pearls turn from white to black; to dust.

Driving home, beneath streetlights the pearls glimpsed and already turning and then she was turning too, quick deliberate reversal and back, streets and streetlights and she did not look at the pearls again, did not stop at the desk to speak to the midnight shift nurse. Instead immediate to his room, no more pearls but the moving eyes so rapid and intense and she bent to him, spoke his name now with such assurance that in the speaking his own lips moved, sluggishly at first but then with surer animation; did he know she was there?

She snapped on the small overhead, aquarium color:

her hands were sweating but absolutely firm. His mouth kept moving, she checked his vital signs; they were very bad. BP and temp, pulse and respiration and after she had charted them, meticulously charted them, she set aside her pen and took up his hand; it was cool, and scarred across the palm, some old scar from the days of light and motion, days of a life now lost to this pitiless vacuum of weakness: held his hand, death's hand in the dark as a mother holds a child, tenderly; tenderly. She said his name, "Elliot," softly in his ear but did not expect recognition, an answer, anything; his lips kept moving, strongly, as if he spoke now through a wind, a torrent, a peeling storm and she said "Elliot" again, the pearls in her pocket between his body and hers and she thought she could hear it, that wind, could almost feel it wash across her own skin, the absolute clarity of cold and his hand now colder, his lips moving in one long grimace, one last powerful rictus and then nothing; silence; no wind at all.

And understanding then, with a calm vouchsafed by Elliot as himself and more than himself, as circumstantial conduit, meant to show her what she was meant to see, to be: angel for the dead, the queen of angels; to accept for and with them, mediatrix, what death is meant to be. Accept as well for herself: angel, finally, of mercy: can she doubt it now, now with his hand in hers, cool and damp as modeling clay and she finds she can go anywhere, feel anything, reach any state she chooses: coma, nirvana, the bright dead bliss of no feeling at all. His lips are heavy, purple as a leathery grape; inside him everything is light, ether and feathers, weightless as tears in the middle of the night and she will stay beside him until the family comes at last, to find him laved and anointed, dead king propped beside her in his cloak of spirit-white, her pocket ripe with pearls of purest darkness turning slow to palest ash; and one beneath her tongue, black and sure and secret as the secret that leads us finally to where at last and always we were always meant to be.

—For Denice

Jubilee

ONCE HEARD it seemed as if she had known the voice forever: exhalation, the sigh of blood through the body, breath's tickle across bare skin; once present, omnipresent since that first time: morning flurry, too-hot bathroom and she brushing her teeth, brushing her hair and as if from the steam in the air itself, the sound of her own name.

I can see you, the voice said.

The tremble of the brush, blunt black bristles and she rigid in pantyhose and high-collared blouse, expensive brown silk blouse wet now at the armpits; no one else in the house, no one there to speak to her and the voice again, soft to her ear: *I can see you* once more but without threat or even insistence, as if sharing a fact meant to bring pleasure to both. The feeling in the air not of presence but of—what? Imminence? Shifting like steam, clouding and dissipating and gone and she now there alone, the brush absurd in one hand as the other braced her upright, the silver molding of the sink digging slightly but painfully into her palm.

I can see you, the voice had said.

No memory, no voice from the grave, from the past to force identity: nothing she had ever heard before. Trembling at the sink, the echo heard somehow in her flesh, the pit of her stomach: staring not into the mirror but at the back of the brush, her hand gripping plastic and: Stop it, she thought, just stop it; and hurrying upstairs to change her stained blouse, fingers forced to competence button by button by will. The thing to do with a thing like this, whatever it was, was to ignore it. Just ignore it: like a bad dream, a bad decision, a bad idea: and it will disappear and go away.

She was thirty-six years old. She had been married for eight years, nine in October, to an art director at a moderately successful publisher of self-help books. Sometimes she wept without knowing precisely why. She had never before heard voices, been visited by the divine, the infernal, the otherworldly; she did not believe in the afterlife or the supernatural; she had not wept nor experienced an orgasm for three months before the voice came to her that first time, came to her as if it had been part of her life forever, came to her as if now inside her would never cease or leave.

She did not tell anyone. She would not have known what to say, how to begin. He talks to me, she could have said, he knows my name. There was no threat in the voice, no reason to fear beyond the fact of its existence; perhaps it was her own response that troubled her. She kept her resolve to do nothing; her husband did not seem to notice her decision nor the inner turbulence prompting it. Her husband did not believe in the supernatural, the hidden vagaries of emotion, the sink and drift of the blood, the echo of one's heart found beating in the breast of another. She was having trouble lubricating when they had sex but he did not seem to notice that either.

Long day, empty day, long wasted lunch with a woman from her department, their talk all triviality: the petty, the brief, job and home, work and love, nothing divided by nothing is what? Silence. Exhausted, straining to see through the rain and the path of faulty wipers, mind empty as an empty cup and: immediate, kiss-moist against her ear, sensation intimate as a hand in an intimate place and *Yours,* the voice said, *oh yours* and her head turning instinctively toward and into the voice, hands on the wheel to follow the motion and the sound of a horn, loud and she swerved back too far like a drunk, like a woman blind, all of it too close: the voice, the car in the next lane, her purse and the big black totebag and all past momentum on the floor, papers, checkbook, notes a grey stew in the spatter of slush, her wet overshoes lying like the fruit of amputation, cut off in the act of escape.

Escape: the voice: was that what it was? He talks to me, to whom could she have said that? Not her husband, not the woman at lunch; why bring it up? to that silent inner stare, why bring it up when you know you don't want to talk about it? But I do want to talk about it, I have to talk about it, I'm going crazy. Crazy people hear voices: the voice of God, the mutterings of angels, the creeping shriek of devils in the dark house of the brain but this was *different,* she had known that from the first, knew it each time: four times, distinct the memory of each occasion, distinct the sound, the feel of the voice: first her name, then the words *I see you;* then *yes,* the voice had said, *yes, oh yes.* And each time—once more in the bathroom, twice in the kitchen, every time alone—the voice accompanied by that feeling of compounding imminence, a certainty so enormous that it was itself impossible, nothing could be so sure. And afterwards hands to face, eyes squeezed shut, reinforcing her corporeality, you are here in this room, you are here in this body in this room. That other is not real. It is not real and not happening... and the afternoon light gone to early darkness, the car around her as real as her own body, to try to speak these things aloud to another human creature was less ultimately possible than the existence of the voice itself. Maybe she should invent an imaginary friend, someone to whom she could tell her troubles; perhaps the voice was the imaginary friend.

Perhaps she was the imaginary friend.

Now her hands, her arms shaking so terribly from reaction that she must at once pull over, settle the car by jerks and choppy braking in the larger puddles at the side of the highway, water down the windshield, her hands loose and trembling in her lap and *Oh yes,* the voice again and with great tenderness, *that's the way it is for you and for me. It's all real; all of it is real.*

"No," in her own anguish, "what do you want?" and she lowered her head against the steering wheel, against the knuckled arch of her shaking hands to feel breath against her cheek and *Real and present,* the voice said. *You and me.*

"Why are you doing this," whispering, eyes closed. Traffic blurring past. Adrenaline for the accident averted, the conflagration still to come and *I speak to you because you can hear me,* said the voice, *you can hear because I speak* and oh that wave of imminence, as if something was not only going to happen but happen now, this minute, an apparition, a hand to reach from empty air to touch her, touch her bent head, stroke her hair and in silence, tears, the bridge past expectancy arcing at last into desire: yes, she thought, pain in her head, pain yoked in her bowstring shoulders like a burden too heavy to bear, *yes* and the touch did not happen: the imminence gone in the white noise of traffic, rooster tail slush and raising her pounding head, opening her eyes: to the end of rush hour and the rain, alone in the driver's seat, arms braced against the steering wheel as if to find purchase in the eye of some deep unknown velocity.

None of it is real. All of it is real.

Wearily hauling the floorboard mess back onto the seat, drip and spatter and pulling back into traffic, confused all at once as to direction—which way? and a line from a song in blunter echo, not the voice but the simpler tones of memory: *It all depends on where you want to go, baby.* Where do you want to go, baby? which way is home?

Clumsy circle at last into the driveway, kitchen light and her husband nodding up as she came in, looking closer and "What's the matter?" pushing back the chair, high back, solid and real: present like the cars on the highway, as a puddle of water, a circle of blood. "What happened? You—"

"I almost had an accident," lying, not-lying, trying to smile back: anything to get out of the kitchen, upstairs to collapse in warmth and cluttered darkness fully clothed across the bed, the muscles in her shoulders aching, present, real. Her body was real.

Yours, oh yours.

What kind of person hears voices? or wants to?

You can hear because I speak.

Sleep was unthinkable but she slept at once, woke when her husband's body touched the bed, his hands touched her body, cool and pleasant, nothing she wanted, nothing real enough to feel and then he was finished and she lay naked and chilled and dreaming, landscapes unremembered, the country of the bodiless and the lost to wake all at once with eyes wide open, cloaked again in imminence stringent as orgasm, unmistakable and *Jubilee,* the voice said and so close she knew for the first time the feel of the breath, its taste absolute against her lips parted to receive it: and said the word back, "Jubilee."

Yes, with such pleasure it bloomed as a smile, her smile brief and dazzled in the dark: *oh yes. Jubilee, your jubilance: you can see it now, can't you.*

"What are you," mouthing the words, her husband indistinct beside her as if unpresent, outside the room and its reality. "What—"

Yours, the voice said; the curve of her jaw as if stroked by a lover's touch; one deep shiver through her skin, grounding throughout her body like a stone thrown in deep water: layers and ripples, circles of response. *Yours, yours.* Her nipples were hard beneath the covers; jubilance: she parted her legs. Breath on her cheek again, her open mouth.

"Touch me," like breath herself.

Yes as if muffled by flesh, the feel of the word against her and the impending touch so charged and so intense that when it happened—light, lighter than breath, each pale and tiny hair rising equally on thigh and nape—she made a little sound, a sound from depths of throat, body, heart, a sound echoed by the whispers, the susurrations of that voice, no words, nothing but sound now in tandem with the touch again: and again, swept without haste or hesitation, boldly up and down her body, belly, legs, breasts, neck, face with closed eyes and open mouth and back down again: and again: and between her legs, open legs, thighs rigid and knees locked and that penetration light and firm and exact, once in in forever, dissolving like sugar in water, disseminating through her body as if it were a drug whose action she could feel, pinpoint through muscle and blood and *Mine,* said the voice in her ear, *mine now* and her orgasm like a sound, a bell in the body, deep dwelling ring felt everywhere, breasts, heart, arching thighs, in the heels of her hands dug silent against the mattress, the attenuated line of her jaw, her open mouth into which, exquisitely, excruciatingly, the smallest touch of moisture, a true kiss on the tip of her tongue and beside her that other body, moving in sleep, muffled in the sheets and blankets and her own heart beating and beating, inner echo like a seashell held to the waiting ear: the sound of the ocean: sea of salt and blood and motion, waves like circles to bring the jubilee.

She woke once more in the night, the dark clear hours of earliest morning to find that she could see through her own body, see down through the sheets and the mattress beneath and the floor beneath that and down and down into dirt and crushed rock and tiny bones: she could see down and up in all directions: she could see many things. Her own testing voice loud as music in her ears, her sigh like a wind from the sea. She could see through the house, every wall a window; she could see patterns of heat and the flickering rise of dust: she could see everything, every-thing, everything but herself: perceived as warmth and silence, perceived in clarity and loss.

She thought she might never close her eyes again.

True morning now and her husband's small coughs and gruntings, rolling over: to emptiness: undisturbed, not sure where she was and he called her name, not loud, called it again. She was not in the bathroom. She was not in the hall. She was not in the kitchen making coffee, she was not on the porch to get the newspaper, her purse like an artifact on the floor beside the sofa and so she had not left the house. He called her name again, not angry, not annoyed, only wondering.

"Anne?"

I'm here, she said. *I'm right here, see? I'm real.*

"Anne?"

Breathing. Her voice in his ear: *I'm here* but he did not seem to hear her although she could hear everything he said, all the words he knew, all the feelings he had ever felt or dreamed of feeling; she saw his dreams like a frieze unrolling, she saw tiny pains and crevices of loss behind his eyes. *I'm right here,* she said again but without urgency; standing quiet and calm and naked in the corner of the room, sunlight across her bare feet, her small sloping breasts, sunlight on and through her, warm and everlasting, no voice but her own in her ears.

"Anne?" in circles, in circling unease growing deeper, she saw, with each revolution, "Anne?" in dishevelment and dismay and then he stopped, stopped where he was, stopped in the light and the morning silence as if he could see, something, see her, see himself and through himself: as if he heard a voice, its own circles deep and rippling deeper in his mind. Unconsciously he touched himself through his pajamas, held his genitals in one considering hand.

"No," he said.

I'm real, she said, and saw both their voices, open as windows above their heads, open as an open mouth, a spread vagina, ready and waiting as a listening ear.

Pas de Deux

SHE LIKED THEM YOUNG, young men; princes. She liked them young when she could like them at all because by now, by this particular minute in time she had had it with older men, clever men, men who always knew what to say, who smiled a certain kind of smile when she talked about passion, about the difference between hunger and love. The young ones didn't smile, or if they did it was with a touching puzzlement because they didn't quite see, weren't sure, didn't fully understand: knowing best what they did not know, that there was still so much to learn.

"Learn what?" Edward's voice from the cage of memory, deep voice, "what's left to learn?" Reaching for the bottle and the glass, pouring for himself. "And who'll do the teaching? You?" That smile like an insect's, like the blank button eyes of a doll made of metal, made from a weapon, born from a knife and see him there, pale sheets crushed careless at the foot of the bed, big canopied bed like a galleon inherited from his first wife—the sheets too, custom-made sheets—all of it given them as a wedding present by his first wife's mother: Adele, her name was and he liked to say it, liked to pretend—was it pretense?—that he had fucked her too, going from mother to daughter in a night, a suite of nights, spreading the seed past four spread legs and prim Alice could never compare, said Edward, with the grand Adele, Adele the former ballet dancer, Adele who had been every-where, lived in Paris and Hong Kong, written a biography of

Balanchine, Adele who wore nothing but black from the day she turned twenty-one and "I don't understand," he would say, head back, knee bent, his short fat cock like some half-eaten sausage, "what you think you can teach me, aren't you being just a little bit absurd?"

"We all have something to learn," she said and he laughed, left the room to return with a book, *Balanchine & Me*—Balanchine in color on the cover, a wee black-and-white of Adele on the back. "Read this," putting the book into her hands. "Find out how much you don't know." Whiskey breath and settling back into bed, glass on his chest, big hairy chest like an animal's, he liked to lie naked with the windows open, lie there and look at her and "Are you cold?" he would say, knowing she was freezing, that her muscles were cramping. "Do you feel a draft?"

No, she could have said, or yes or fuck you or a million other responses but in the end she had made none of them, said nothing, got out. Left him there in his canopied bed and found her own place, her own space, living above her studio: dance studio, she had been away for a long time but now she was back and soon, another month or two she would have enough money maybe to keep the heat on all the time, keep the lights on, keep going. *Keep on going:* that was her word now, her world, motion at any cost. She was too old to be a dancer? had been away too long, forgotten too much, lost the fascistic grace of the body in torment, the body as tool of motion, of the will? *No.* As long as she had legs, arms, a back to bend or twist, as long as she could move she could dance.

Alone.

In the cold.

In the dark.

Pas de Deux

Sometimes when it got too dark even for her she would leave, head off to the clubs where for the price of a beer she could dance all night to thrash or steelcore, a dance different from the work she did at the barre: jerked and slammed past exhaustion, hair stuck slick to her face, shirt stuck to her body, slapping water on her neck in the lavatory through the smoke and stink and back out with her head down, eyes closed, body fierce and martyred by the motion; incredible to watch, she knew it, people told her; men told her, following her as she stalked off the floor, leaning close to her stool at the bar and they said she was terrific, a terrific dancer; and closer, closer still the question inevitable, itself a step in the dance: why was she dancing alone? "You need a partner," but of course that was not possible, not really because there was no one she wanted, no one who could do what she could do and so she would shrug, smile sometimes but mostly not, shrug and shake her head and "No," turning her face away. "No thanks."

Sometimes they bought her drinks, sometimes she drank them; sometimes, if they were young enough, kind enough, she would take them home, up past the studio to the flat with its half-strung blinds and rickety futon, unsquared piles of dance magazines, old toe shoes and bloody wraps and she would fuck them, slowly or quickly, in silence or with little panting yelps or cries like a dog's, head back in the darkness and the blurred sound of the space heater like an engine running, running itself breathless and empty and dry. Afterwards she would lie beside them, up on one elbow and talk, tell them about dancing, about passion, about the difference between hunger and love and there in the dark, the rising and falling of her voice processional as water, as music, lying there in the moist warmth created by their bodies they were moved—by her words, by her body—to create it anew, make the bridge between love and hunger: they were young, they could go all night. And then they would look up at her and "You're beautiful," they said, they all said it. "You're so beautiful, can I call you?"

"Sure," she would say. "Sure, you can call me," leaning over them, breathing slowed, the sweat on her breasts drying to a thin prickle and see their faces, watch them smile, see them dress—jeans and T-shirts, ripped vests and camouflage coats, bandannas on their heads, tiny little earrings in silver and gold—and watch them go and before they go give them the number, press it into their hands; the number of the cleaner's where she used to take Edward's suits but how was it cruel, she asked herself, told herself, how was it wrong not to offer what she did not have? Far worse to pretend, string them along when she knew that she had already given all she had to give, one night, her discourse, she never took the same one twice and there were always so many, so many clubs, so many bars in this city of bars and clubs, lights in the darkness, the bottle as cold as knowledge in her warm and slippery grasp.

Sometimes she walked home, from the bars and the clubs; it was nothing for her to walk ten, thirty, fifty blocks, no one ever bothered her, she always walked alone. Head down, hands at her sides like a felon, a movie criminal, *just keep walking* through darkness, four AM rain or the last fine scornful drift of snow, ice like cosmetics to powder her face, chill to gel the sweat in her hair, short hair, Edward said she looked like a lifer: "What were you in for?" as she stood ruffling her hair in the bathroom mirror, sifting out the loose snips, dead curls and his image sideways in the glass as if distorted, past focus, in flux. "You don't have the facial structure for a cut like that," one-hand reaching to turn her face, aim it towards the light like a gun above; that smile, like an abdicated king's. "Once Alice cut her hair off, all her hair, to spite me; she denied it, said she only wanted a different look but I knew her, I knew that's what it was. Adele," the name as always honey in his mouth, "knew too, and she cut off *her* hair to spite Alice. Of course *she* looked terrific, really sexy and butch, but she had the face for it. Bone structure," almost kindly to her, patting her face with both hands, patty-cake, baby face, squeezing her cheeks in the mirror. "That's what you don't have."

And now this cold walk, each individual bone in her face aching, teeth aching, sound of the wind in her ears even when she was safe inside, door locked, space heater's orange drone and as late as it was, as cold as it was she stripped down to leggings, bare feet, bare breasts and danced in the dark, sweating, panting, the stitch cruel in her side, in her throat, in her heart, tripped by unseen obstacles, one hip slamming hard into the barre, metallic thud of metal to flesh, flesh to metal like mating, like fucking and she wished she had brought someone home with her, it would have been nice to fuck a warm boy in the dark but she was alone and so she danced instead, spun and stumbled and hit the barre, hit the barre, hit the barre until she literally could not move, stood knees locked and panting, panting from fear of stasis as outside, past the yellowed shades, the sun at last began to rise.

Adele's book lay where she had tossed it, square and silent on the bathroom floor but one night, back from dancing and sick to her stomach—the beer, something had not agreed with her—from the toilet she picked it up, skimmed through the chapters, the inset pictures and although it was very poorly written—as a writer Adele had apparently been a fine dancer—still there was something, one phrase arresting like a blow, a slap in the face: "For me," said Adele, "Balanchine was a prince. You must find your own prince, you must make him your own."

Find your prince: Prince Edward! and she laughed, pants rucked down around her ankles, thin yellow diarrhea and she laughed and laughed but the phrase stayed with her, clung like the memory of motion to the bones and she began to look, here and there, at the young men at the clubs, look and gauge and wonder and sometimes at night, pinned and breathing beneath them, talking of hunger and love she would wonder what a prince was, how to see one: how one knew: was it something in the body, some burn, some vast unspeaking signal? The body does not lie: she knew this. And Adele—considering the small black-and-white picture, that arched avian nose, high bones to show like a taunt to life itself the skull inside the meat—had more than likely known it too.

The body does not lie.

Ten years old on the way to ballet class, forced by her mother's instigation: "So you'll learn how to move, sweetie," her mother so small and fat and anxious, patting her daughter's cheeks, round cheeks, small bony chin like a misplaced fist. "So you'll be more comfortable with your body."

"But I am comfortable," sullen child's lie, head averted, temple pressed stubborn to the hot glass of the car window. "Anyway I'd rather play soccer, why can't I sign up for soccer?"

"Dance is better," the old car swung inexpertly into the strip mall parking lot, Dance Academy in stylized curlicue blue, cheap rice-paper blinds between Mindy's Dog Grooming and a discount hand-tool outlet. Smaller inside than it seemed from the street, ferocious dry air-conditioned cold and three girls listless at the barre, two older than she, one much younger, all in cotton-candy colors; from past the walls the sounds of barking dogs. The woman at the desk asking "Will this be for the full semester?" and her mother's diffidence, well we just wanted to try the introductory sessions, just let her try and see if she—

"I don't want to dance," her own voice, not loud but the girls looked up, all of them, starlings on a branch, prisoners in a cell. "I want to play soccer."

The woman's gaze; she did not bother to smile. "Oh no," she said. "No sports for you, you've got a dancer's body."

"Are you a dancer?" Shouted into her ear, that eager young voice. "I mean like professionally?"

"Yes," she said. "No."

"Can I buy you a drink? What're you drinking?" and it was one beer, then two, then six and they stopped on the way to her place, stopped and bought a bottle of VO—a princely gesture?—and sat in the dark doing shots as he undressed her, stripped like skin the moist drape of her T-shirt, her Spartan white panties, her black cotton skirt till she sat naked and drunk and shivering, her nipples hard, all the light gone from the room and "The way you move," he said, kept saying, hushed voice of glimpsed marvels. "Wow. The way you *move,* I knew right away you were some kind of dancer, right, I mean like for a living. Are you in the ballet? Are you—"

"Here," she said, "here, I'll show you," and downstairs, hand in hand and naked in the dark, the lessening angle of his erection but he was young and it was easy, one or two or six little pulls and he was stiff as a board, as a barre, stiff and ready and she danced for him first, danced around him, Salome without the veils: rubbing her breasts against his back, trapping his thighs with her own and since he was drunk it took longer but not so very long, not much time after all before they were lying there, warmth's illusion and panting into one another's mouths and she told him the difference between love and hunger, between what is needed and what must be had and "You're so beautiful," he said, slurred words and a smile of great simplicity, a deep and tender smile; it was doubtful he had heard anything she had said. His penis against her like a finger, the touch confiding: "So can I, can I call you?"

Dust, grains of dirt stuck to her skin, to the skin of her face against the floor. No prince: or not for her: her body said so. "Sure," she said. "Sure, you can call me."

When he had gone she went back upstairs, took up Adele's book, and began again to read it page by page.

No more ballet classes, dancer's body or no she was out and now it was too late for tap or modern dance, too late for soccer and so she spent the summer with her father, dragging up and down the four flights of his walk-up, silent and staring at the TV, "Why don't you go out?" Lighting up a menthol cigarette, he smoked three-and-a-half packs a day; by the time she was eighteen he would be dead. "Meet some kids or something."

"There aren't any kids in this building," she said. A musical on TV, the Arts in America channel; two women singing about travel and trains. "And it's too hot to go out." The air conditioner worked but not well; endless the scent of mildew and smoke, of her father's aftershave when he dressed to go out: "Keep the door locked," as he left, to whom would she open it anyway? Sitting up by the TV, chin in hand in the constant draft, the sound of traffic outside.

Pas de Deux

In September he sent her back to her mother, back to school; she never went to a dance class again.

"It's a part-time position," the woman said. She might have been twenty, very dark skin, very dark eyes; severe, like a young Martha Graham. "The students—we have a full class load now— "

"How many?"

"Fifty."

Fifty dancers, all much younger than she, all fierce, committed, ambitious. Toe shoes and a shower, the smell of hand cream, the smell of warm bodies: glossy floors and mirrors, mirrors everywhere, the harder gloss of the barre and *no*, a voice like Adele's in her head, *you cannot do this:* "No," she said, rising, pushing out of the chair so it almost tipped, so she almost fell. "No, I can't, I can't teach a class right now."

"It's not a teaching position," sternly, "it's an *assistant's*—"

Keep the shower room clean, keep the records, help them warm up, watch them dance, no, oh no. "Oh no," as she walked home, hands at her sides, what were you in for? Life: a lifer. Edward's number was still in her book, still written in black ink. She could not keep both the studio and the flat: the futon, the dance magazines, her unconnected telephone all moved downstairs, shoved in a corner, away from the barre. Sometimes the toilet didn't flush. The young men never seemed to mind.

Adele's book lay beneath her pillow, Balanchine's face turned down like an unwanted jack, prince of hearts, king of staves: and upturned black-and-white Adele, pinched nose and constant stare, Our Lady of Perpetual Motion.

"You look awful," Edward said, stern as the young woman had been, there behind her desk: there in the restaurant, staring at her. "Did you know that? Completely haggard."

"Money," she said. "I need to borrow some money."

"You're in no position to pay it back."

"No," she said. "I'm not. Not now. But when I—"

"You must be crazy," he said and ordered for them both, cream of leek-and-tarragon soup, some kind of fish. White wine. The server looked at her strangely; Adele could be heard to laugh, a little laugh inhuman, clockwork wound the wrong way. "Where are you living now, in a dumpster?"

She would not say; she would not show him. He wanted to fuck, afterwards, after dinner but she wouldn't do that either, arms crossed and mute and "Where's all this from, anyway?" pushing back at the sheets, seemingly serene, not disappointed; his erection looked smaller somehow, fat but weak like a toothless snake, like a worm. The rooms were so warm, the bedroom as hot as a beating heart; the big bed still looked like a galleon, sheets and hangings cherry-red and "All this devotion," he said. "Suffering for your art. You never gave much of a shit about ballet, about dance when I knew you."

That's not true but she didn't say it, how explain anything to him? and ballet of course brought up Adele: "You've never even read her book on Balanchine," scratching his testicles. "If you cared about dance at all, you would."

He was always a fool, advised Adele: *find your prince* and "I need the money now," she said. "Tonight," and to her surprise he gave it to her, right then, in cash; how rich he must be, to give so much so casually. Putting it into her hands, closing her fingers around it and "Now suck me," he said. Standing there naked, his cock begun at last to stir. "That's right, be a good girl, suck me off."

She said nothing.

"Or I'll take the money back."

The bills were warm, warm as the room around her, warm as his hand around her own and in one motion she brought their linked hands, his own hand topmost to rise, fast and sharp to smash under his chin, hit so hard his hand jerked open, her hand free, the bills falling to the floor and gone then, shoving out the door with her fingers stinging and burning, burning in the cold outside.

Adele was silent.

"Do you—" One of the young ones, crouched between her legs, her canted knees on the futon with its one wrinkled sheet, its coverlet faded to the color of sand. "Do you have condoms? Because I don't."

"No," she said. "I don't either."

His lower lip thrust out like a child defrauded, a pouting child. "Well then what're we going to do?"

"Dance," she said. "We can dance."

She got a job at a used bookstore, erratic schedule, the hours nobody wanted and every hour, every minute a chafe, an itch unbearable to stand so still this way, medical textbooks and romance novels, celebrity bios and how-to books—once even *Balanchine & Me*, which she instantly stuffed into her backpack without thinking twice; why not? it was hers already and this a better copy, the photograph sharper, the pages not bent and soft and torn—taking money across the counter and she knew it was wrong, she knew it was not the right thing to do but sometimes she overcharged for the books, not much, a dollar here or there and pocketed the money, kept the change, what else could she do? The job paid nothing and took so much, stole time which she needed, had to have: no studio would hire her, no company until she was good enough, professional enough to teach and she had missed so much, lost so much time: she had to make up, catch up, keep working and there were only so many hours in the day, already she woke at six to dance before work, work all day and then out to the clubs at night for that other dancing that while exhausting somehow refreshed her, made her new again, ready to dance again so what else was there to do?

And sometimes—she did not like this either, but her world was full, now, of things she could not like—she let the young men buy things for her, breakfast, a bag of dough-nuts, carryout coffee which she drank later, cold coffee in the cold, walking to work at the bookstore and then some-how they found out about the stealing, she never knew how but they did and they fired her, kept her last week's wages to pay for what she had taken and that night she danced as if she were dying, flailing arms and her head swinging in cir-cles, she felt as if her neck would snap, wanted it to snap, break and let her head go flying to smash red and grey to silence against the wall: *no prince for you*, nothing, nothing from Adele even though she asked: *what would you do? tell me, I need to know, I have to know what to do* and after-wards, alone and panting by the bar from which she could not afford to buy a drink, approached not by one of the young men, no prince but someone else, an older man in black jeans and a jacket who told her she was one terrific dancer, really sexy, and if she was interested he had a proposition to make.

"Naked?"

"Private parties," he said. The smell of menthol ciga-rettes, a red leather couch above which hung a series of Nagle nudes and "They never touch you, never. That's not in the contract, I'm not paying you for that. They're not paying *me* for that." Gazing at her as if she were already naked. "You ever wear makeup? You could stand a little lipstick. Do something with your hair, too, maybe."

"How much?" she asked, and he told her.

Silence.

"When?" she asked, and he told her that too.

Too-loud music, she brought her own tape player and a selection of tapes, twenty-two different choices from *The Stripper* to soft rock to thrash, she could dance to anything and it didn't matter as much as she had feared, being naked, not as bad as it might have been although at first it was terrible, the things they said, they were so different from the young men at the clubs, being naked must make the difference but after awhile there was no difference after all or perhaps she had forgotten how to listen, forgotten everything but the feel of the music and that had not changed, the music and the sweat and the muscles in her body, dancer's muscles and she did four parties a night, six on a good night; one night she did ten but that was too much, she had almost fallen off the table, almost broken her arm on a chair's unpadded back and with that much work she had no time for herself, for the real dancing, alone at the barre, alone in the dark and the winter, it seemed, would last forever, her hands were always frozen, broken windows in her studio and she covered them over with cardboard and duct tape, covered them over with shaking hands and her hands, she thought, were growing thinner or perhaps her fingers were longer, it was hard to tell, always so dark in here but she thought she might have lost some weight, a few pounds, five or ten and at the parties they called her skinny, or scrawny, "get your scrawny ass movin', babe" or "hey where's your tits?" but she had gone past the point of listening, of caring; had discovered that she would never discover her prince in places like this, her partner, the one she had to have: *find your prince* and although Adele made less sense these days, spoke less frequently still she was the only one who understood: the new copy gone to rags like the old one, reading between the lines and while she talked very little about her own life—it was a biography of Balanchine after all—still some of her insights, her guesses and pains emerged and in the reading emerged anew: Adele's like me, she thought, reading certain passages again and again, she knows what it's like to need to dance, to push the need away and away like an importunate lover, like a prince only to seek it again with broken hands and a broken body, seek it because it is the only thing you need: the difference between love and hunger: *find your prince* and find a partner, because no one can dance forever alone.

Different clubs now in this endless winter, places she had never been, streets she had once avoided but she could not go back to some of the old places, too many young men there whose faces she knew, whose bodies she knew, who could never be her prince and something told her to hurry: time tumbling and burning, time seeping away and it was Adele's voice in her head, snatches of the book, passages mumbled by memory so often they took on the force of prayer, of chant, plainsong garbled by beating blood in the head as she danced, as she danced, as she danced: and the young men did not approach as often or with such enthusiasm although her dance was still superb, even better now than it had ever been; sometimes she caught them staring, walking off the floor and they would turn their heads, look away, did they think she had not seen? Eyes closed still she knew: *the body does not lie* but the ones who did speak, who did approach were different now, a fundamental change: "Hey," no smile, wary hand on the drink. "You with anybody?"

I am looking for a prince. "No," she would say, surface calm and back at her place—it was the one rule on which she insisted, she would not go to them—the rigor of vision, letting the body decide—

"You got a rubber?"

"No."

—and again and again the same report, no prince and no partner and indifferent she would slide away, sometimes they had not even finished, were still thrashing and gulping but these owned not even the promise of kindness and so were owed no kindness in return: indifferent she shoved them away, pushed them off and most grew angry, a few of them threatened to hit her, one or two of them did but in the end they cursed, they dressed, they left and she was left alone, pinprick lights through the cold cardboard, sweet uneasy smell from the space-heater coils: bending and flexing her feet and her fingers, all pared far past mere meat to show the stretch and grace of tendon, the uncompromising structure of the bone.

A weekend's worth of frat parties, at one place they threw beer on her, at another they jeered because she was so thin and would not let her dance, sent her away: it was happening more and more now, she might do two parties a night, one, sometimes there were no calls for her at all. In the office with the Nagle prints: "What are you, anorexic or something? I don't deal, you know, in freaks, I don't want that trade. You want to keep dancing, you better start eating."

What he did not understand, of course, what Adele understood superbly was that the meat was not necessary, in fact became a mere impediment to motion: see how much more easily she turned, how firmly in command of space, of vertical distance—*ballon,* dancers called it, that aerial quality also called elevation—how wedded she was to motion when there was less of the body to carry? Why sacrifice that for the desire of fools?

"You must weigh ninety pounds."

She shrugged.

"Anyway you're lucky. There's a party next weekend, some kind of farewell party, the guy picked you out of the picture book. You especially he said he wants."

She shrugged again.

"He wants you early, maybe a little extra-special dance— no touching, he knows that, but it's like a present for the guest of honor, right? So be there by eight," handing her one of the go-to cards, a 3 x 5 with an address and phone number.

Edward's address.

"Hey, I need a, I need a rubber or something. You got something?"

"No."

"Hey, you're—you're, like, *bleeding* down there, are you on the rag or something?"

No answer.

"You should have taken the money," Edward said, watching her walk in: the faux library, books unread, shelves full of silly crystal frogs, squat jade warriors, girls with ruby eyes. "You look even worse than you did the last time I saw you, even worse than that ugly Polaroid in the book.... I can't imagine you're getting much business; are you? Is this your idea of professional dance?"

She shrugged.

"Given up on the ballet?" and pouring wine, one glass; then shrugging and pouring another, go on, help yourself.

188

The hired help. Like a maid, or a delivery boy; a prostitute. "The man I spoke to said you don't have sex with your clients—is that true?"

"I dance," she said. The room looked exactly the same, same quality of light, same smells; in the bedroom, on the bed the sheets would be red, and slick, and soft. "I show up and I dance."

"Naked."

"In a G-string."

"'Air on a G-String,'" sipping his wine. "Can you dance to that? Does it have a good beat? *Christ,*" with real distaste as she removed her coat, "look at you. You need a doctor, you're nothing but bones."

"Is there a party?" she said. "Or did you make that up?"

"No, there's a party but it's not here, not tonight. Tonight you can dance for me; if you're good I'll even tip you . . . is tipping permitted? or is it added on to the bill?"

She said nothing. She was thinking of Adele, Adele here in these rooms, choosing the bed linens, choosing the bed on which, Edward boasted, the two of them had made love before the wedding, before he and daughter Alice were even formally engaged: the way her body moved, he had said, it was unbelievable and "Tell me about Adele," she said, sting of wine on her lips, on the sores inside her mouth. Thread of blood in the pale wine. "When was the last time you saw her?"

"What does that have to do with anything?"

"Just tell me," she said.

It was here, he said, she was in town and we met for dinner, some Swedish restaurant, only four or five tables, best-kept secret in town but of course she knew, she always knew about everything. "And after dinner we came back home," he said. "To our bed."

"How old was she then?"

"What difference can that possibly make?"

"How old was she?"

"You know, looking at you now it's hard to believe I ever touched you. I certainly wouldn't want to touch you now."

"How old was she?" and he told her, confirming what she had already known: like herself and the young men, the would-be princes, the parallel held true and there on one of the shelves—how had she missed it? a photograph of Adele, Adele at thirty maybe or maybe slightly older, that pinched stare relaxed now into the gaze of the true Medusa, queen of an older motion, sinuous and rapt and "Finish your drink," Edward said; his voice came to her as if from far away, the way Adele had used to sound. "Finish your drink and you can go."

Shall I go? to the picture of Adele who without perceptibly moving her lips said *no, no you must not go, that is the one thing you must not do* and bending, she took up the book, *Balanchine & Me* from the bag where the tapes were, the music, she had her own music tonight, Adele's humming voice in her head and "Take a look," she said to Edward, gaily, almost smiling, "take a look," and she began to strip, shoes and stockings, skirt and blouse, each piece shed deliberate as a blow and "You're sick," Edward said; he did not want to look at her. "You're very sick, you ought to see a doctor."

"I don't need a doctor." Bra off, her flat breasts like airless pancakes, like starving people on TV and without music, without sound she began to dance: not the party-dances, not even what she did alone with the barre but something different, more basic, closer to the heart of the bone and as she danced—panting, sweat down her sides and her face, sweat in her mouth and Edward standing glass in hand, staring and staring and she talked about the prince, the prince and the partner and all her seeking, all her lost and wandering ways: was she talking out loud? and then to the picture, the photograph of Adele: does he know? can he learn, will he ever understand?

The body does not lie, said Adele. *But he is trapped in his body. He was always there, for me, for you but he is trapped, he needs to get out. I could not help him get out so now you must. Get him out* and "Get out," he said: her whirling body, one leg high, high, even with her shoulder, look at those tendons, that flex and stretch! The difference between lead and air, meat and feathers, hunger and love and "Listen now," she said: listen now and the little picture of Adele lit up, bloomed as if light rose from within, lit outward from the heart and with both hands she grabbed for the figurines, jade and crystal, frog and solider and threw them to the floor, at the walls, up and down to smash and glitter, topple and fall and, shouting, he grabbed for her, tried to take her hands, tried to join the dance but *he is trapped* and "I know," she said to Adele, the glowing picture, "oh I know," and when he came for her again she hit him as hard as she could with the ball of her foot, karate kick, fierce and sure in the crotch to make him go down, fall, lie cramped and curled on the silence of the floor, curled about the red worm of his cock, the cradle of his balls: like a worm caught on the sidewalk, curling in panic in the absence of the earth.

The body does not lie, said Adele.

Edward gasping, a wet, weeping sound and she kicked him again, harder this time, a slow deliberate kick: *En pointe,* she said with a smile to the picture, and with one finger hooked the G-string from the cresting pelvic arch.

Bondage

SHE WAS SHAPED LIKE SCULPTURE: high bones, high forehead, long fingers silver-cool against his skin as they lay side by side in the deep four-poster, princess bed draped in lace and gauze and "Don't ever buy me a ring," she said; those fingers on his belly, up and down, up and down, tickling in his navel, playing with his balls. "I don't like them."

Even her voice, as calm and sure as metal. "Why not?" he said.

"They're just—" Fingertips, nipping at his thighs. "They're bondage gear."

"Bondage, sure. Like a wedding band, right?"

And her shrug, half a smile, one-elbow rise to reach for her drink: that long white back, faint skeleton trail of bones and "What do you know about bondage?" her smile wider now, canine flash. "B&D, S&M. You ever do that, any of that?"

Have you? "No," he said. "I'm not into pain."

"It's not about pain," she said, "or anyway it doesn't have to be. Bondage and discipline," tapping his chest for emphasis. "Who's on top." She drank what was left in the glass, set it back on the floor, climbed atop him so her breasts were inches from his mouth. "Like now," she said.

Her taste of perfume, of faintest salt: long legs hooked high above his hips, strong and growing stronger, wilder as she rode him, head straining back, back, as if she would twist that long white body into a circle, bend it like sculpture, like metal and stone and when he came it was too soon, fast and over and she was looking at him and almost smiling, lips spread to show those little pointed teeth.

"Not so bad, was it?" she said. "Woman superior?"

"But that's not the same thing," he said, still breathless. "Not the same thing at all."

Next day's dinner, some Tex-Mex place she loved: plastic cacti, the waiters in ten-gallon hats and reaching for her bag beneath the table, reaching and: a box, gift box embossed black on black, Secret Pleasures and "Here," she said with half a smile. "For you."

"What's this for?" he said.

"No reason—go on, open it," and he did, something soft and limp inside and, curious, he unfolded that softness, spread it flat on the table between them: supple white leather oval, no true eyes, gill-slit where the mouth should be and "Pretty cool, isn't it?" she said. Tangle of black strings, one black grommet on each side, simple as desire itself. "Do you like it?"

"Where'd you get this?" The box in hand again, examination and "From a sex store," she said, "downtown. Thumb cuffs and cock rings, nipple clamps. Piercing jewelry." Touching the mask. "And these."

And a server there to refill their water glasses, frank stare at the mask on the table: "What's that?" Eighteen, nineteen years old, faint drift of acne across his forehead beneath the ludicrous hat. "For Halloween?"

"No," she said before he could speak, "no, it's for sex. A sex toy," and the boy laughed a little, hasty to fill the glasses and be gone and "Why'd you have to say that?" he said, annoyed. At the work station see the boy with another server, their tandem turn to stare and she laughed, reached to take the mask and place it back inside the box.

"No reason," she said. "Just part of the game."

And later in bed, kisses and nipping fingers, playful hands on his thighs but he was waiting, he knew it would come and: reaching for her glass she retrieved as well the box, Secret Pleasures and the featureless face within, white face waiting for flesh to fill it, carry it, make it move and "Go on," she said, "I bought it for you, put it on."

"I will if you will."

"You first," and she helped him adjust it, tie the dangle of strings so the mask lay comfortably close, leather so soft it might have been a second skin: *Who am I?* wiped clean of all expression, no mouth to sulk or smile and "Mmmmm," her hands now on his face, petting, stroking the mask. "You should see how you look."

"I look like nothing," he said. Strange to feel the movement of muscles when he spoke, feel his lips against the mask like some alien skin. "Everyman."

"The bogeyman," and she laughed, leaning back, back against the pillows, cheekbone flush and reaching, reaching to bring his face to her breasts: "Your turn," she said. "Your turn to be on top."

It grew hot, inside the mask; he didn't mind.

"Your turn." Raining outside, monotony of thunder and she crabby in quilts, ugly nightgown and "Your turn," he said again, dangling the mask by its strings: caul from some secret birth, some unborn self and "Go on," he said, feeling his hard-on press his trousers as facial bones might press the mask: a slight straining, the pressure of rising heat and the mask did not fit her quite as well, hung slightly beneath her chin but he tightened the strings again—"Ow," more annoyance than real pain, her voice softer somehow because dampered, muffled by the slit which did not completely meet her lips. "It's too tight," faint her voice but he left it that way, no portion of her features visible, nothing but faceless white.

"Lie down," he said.

"Oh, not here," yet without true complaint, she was not attending, she was feeling the mask with her fingers, curious to press against cheekbones and chin and "You know I tried this on before," more than half to herself. "But not so—"

"Lie down," he said; he was already naked. Thunder like the echo of a beating heart, giant's heart in rhythm with his own; pulse of blood and rain on the roof, a clutch of claws, her body bent obedient on the landscape of the quilts: and afterwards, half-turned from him: "You hurt me," she said, touching herself, pale hands between her legs. "Don't be so rough."

The mask on the floor like a self discarded; no one; anyone. Everyman. "I'm sorry," he said. "I didn't mean to."

The next time he lay below her, masked and silent: *don't move*, that was the game, *no matter what don't move*: clamped thighs, her juddering breasts and she bit him, bright teeth in the shoulder hard enough to leave a bruise: nipping and pinching with her nails, scratches on his chest, his back and he had to fight not to shift or move, not to push her away, to lay absolutely still even as he came, sweep of red pleasure and she above in reckless motion, hair sweat-wild and tumbled, panting as if she had no air and "Oh, yes," collapsing down to lie beside him, one leg stretched companionably across his two, thigh high on his hip and without moving anything but his fingers he pinched her, quick and brutal on her inner thigh and

in perfect reflex she slapped him, very hard, across the face, both sound and impact deadened by the presence of the mask.

Neither spoke.

Some time after that he fell asleep, woke much later to find her curled far across the bed and himself still in the mask: sweat dried to an itch across his cheekbones, the differing itch of his overnight beard, fingers clumsy with fatigue against the strings.

Waking to true morning he found it crumpled on the floor, spoor and element of dream made to follow the sleeper all the way to the waking world.

"I'm sorry," she said. She might have been crying, earlier, in the shower; she had kept the bathroom door closed; her eyes were clear but swollen, pink and sore around the lids. "I never meant to hit you."

I'm sorry too. "Let's forget it," he said. "OK?"

The next time they made love they did not use the mask: plain faces, closed eyes and although it was good (with her it was almost always good) still he missed it, the heat within that stasis, visible and not, here and not-here: but said nothing, did not mention it at all.

He wondered if she missed it, too.

Dinner: carryout Thai in little lumps, he had waited too long to leave the office, stuck twice in traffic in a heavy storm; so much rain, lately. The food on his plate gone slick and cold, eating alone, clicking through channels and outside another sound, her car in the driveway: half-rising to open the door, let her in and "Hi," wet and breathless, hair stuck to her face, raincoat spatter and "Oh good," she said, "you got dinner." Side by side on the sofa and now that she was home he opened a bottle of wine, two bottles, still on the sofa and he started to undress her, blouse and bra, hooks and eyes and "Wait," she said, voice lightly slurred and warm from the wine. "Just wait a minute," and gone then as he stripped, lay back on the sofa, rain on the roof and all at once the white face, peering at him, mouth expressionless but beneath, he knew, a smile.

"Peekaboo," she said and inside him the sudden surge, heat pure and rising like mercury, like the tempo of the storm and "Let me wear it," he said, up on one elbow, rising to reach for the strings, "and then you can—"

"No," from above him, pale and remote. "It's not your turn."

That stare: he could not see her eyes and inside him then a differing surge, something grey and chilly, like metal, like falling rain.

Secret Pleasures: between a video store and a deli, glass door opaque and inside the ratchet and thump of industrial music, steel-toned racks to display the shiny harnesses, leather hoods and thigh-high boots and below the counter a glass case of jewelry, piercing jewelry like little iron bars, dumbbells, hooks and circles and "Can I help you?" from a tall thin boy in leather, boots and jacket, head to toe and "Masks," he said. "I want to see the masks," and after all it was very easy to say, no doubt the clerks had already seen it all, this boy with his thin cheeks and ragged hair leading him to the display carousel, to show him what there was to see: buckles and loops and ribbon ties, leather and rubber all faces he might wear, desires he might claim